Holding It Down: A Love

By NFINITEE BLAYZE

For every person who ever loved through the storm and came out shining.

Chapter 1 – Searching for Something Real

The rain had been falling since dusk, a steady whisper that pressed against the window like a secret trying to get in. Layla pulled her blanket tighter around her shoulders and let her eyes follow the thin silver trails sliding down the glass. The apartment was quiet except for the low hum of the refrigerator and the muted bass of a car somewhere outside. She'd turned the television off an hour ago—every commercial break, every empty sitcom laugh, had felt like noise she couldn't stand tonight.Her phone lit up again on the coffee table. "You up?"The words blinked at her through the blue glow. Same number, same kind of message, same disappointment already curling in her stomach. She locked the screen and tossed the phone onto the couch cushion beside her. "Always the same story," she murmured.Her own voice sounded foreign in the stillness. She leaned back, exhaling slow, trying to quiet the storm inside that was louder than the one outside.Layla had learned a lot about heartbreak. It didn't always come with shouting or betrayal. Sometimes it came with silence—the kind that stretched between text messages, the kind that said you care more than I do without ever needing words. Three years of trying, three relationships that started with hope and ended with excuses.The last one, David, had seemed different. He'd brought her lunch to the clinic, remembered her birthday, talked about meeting Mayah. Then one morning he'd simply stopped calling. No fight, no closure. Just absence. After that, Layla promised herself she'd stop chasing what didn't want to be caught.She tried to keep busy instead. The community clinic where she worked always needed more hands. She was good at her job—steady, efficient, the one who could coax a smile out of nervous patients and keep her coworkers calm when the waiting room overflowed. But lately even that sense of purpose had started to thin. Some nights she'd come home, drop her purse on the counter, and wonder if this was it—if life would always be a loop of work, bills, and lonely evenings filled with half-hearted messages from men who only wanted a distraction.A door creaked down the hallway. "A'Laylah?" Mayah's voice was soft, still thick with sleep. "Yeah, baby?" "You okay?" The teenager stepped into the dim light of the living room, her messy bun lopsided, oversized T-shirt slipping off one shoulder. She looked like a smaller version of their mother—same almond eyes, same stubborn set of the jaw. Layla forced a smile. "I'm fine. Couldn't sleep." Maya dropped onto the couch beside her. "You stressing again?" "Maybe a little." Mayah eyed the phone face-down on the cushion. "That dude texting you again?" Layla chuckled. "You too nosy." "I'm just saying," Mayah said, drawing her knees up. "You deserve somebody that texts more than two words." "That's a low bar," Layla laughed, shaking her head. Mayah shrugged. "Then raise it. You too good for weak energy." Layla stared at her baby sister, amused and proud all at once. "When did you get so grown?" "Since I started watching you put everyone else first." The honesty in Mayah's tone landed like a gentle punch. Layla leaned over and kissed her forehead. "Go on back to bed, little philosopher." "Fine," Mayah said, standing. "But remember what I said. Don't let nobody waste your time." "I'll try," Layla promised. When the bedroom door closed again, she whispered to the empty room, "I just want something real."

It slipped out like a prayer.She didn't know that prayer was already in motion.A week later the world smelled like charcoal and summer heat. Tasha's call had come at just the right time—Girl, you been in that house too long. Come eat some ribs and remember you still cute.Layla had resisted, then finally caved. She spent the morning twisting her hair and ironing the yellow sundress she hadn't worn since last summer. It felt like sunshine against her skin.When she reached Big Mike's backyard, music and laughter filled the air. The grill smoked like an altar to good times. Children chased each other with water guns, women gossiped over paper plates, men argued about football. It smelled like family, even if most people there weren't related.Layla eased into the rhythm, sipping sweet tea and letting herself breathe. For the first time in weeks, she wasn't thinking about bills or heartbreak.Then she saw him.Marcus stood near the grill, tall and broad-shouldered, the heat from the coals drawing a shimmer around him. He wore a black tee, gray joggers, and an easy stillness that made the noise around him fade. He laughed at something one of the kids said, the sound low and warm.When their eyes met, it wasn't long—but long enough for her pulse to skip.Tasha nudged her. "You see what I see?"Layla tried to act unbothered. "What you talking about?" "That's Marcus," Tasha whispered. "Darnell's cousin. Just moved back from Atlanta. Real good guy. You want me to—" "No," Layla said quickly, but she was smiling. "Don't start." Tasha grinned. "Too late." A few minutes later, Marcus walked over carrying two paper plates loaded with barbecue. "Marcus said you might want some of this," he said, voice deep enough to rumble. "I made the sauce." Layla raised an eyebrow. "You made it?" "Yeah, why?" "What if it's nasty?" He laughed—a sound that felt like a hug. "Then I guess I owe you dinner somewhere else to make up for it." She tasted a forkful just to play along. Sweet, smoky, with a slow heat that lingered. "Okay," she said, nodding. "You might know what you're doing." "Told you." He smiled, extending a hand. "I'm Marcus." "Layla." Their hands met—warm, steady, and for a moment, neither of them pulled away. They drifted toward a picnic table beneath the big oak tree that shaded half the yard. The wood was rough beneath their elbows, and somebody's playlist switched from upbeat trap to 90s R&B. Layla relaxed a little; the soft rhythm fit her mood better. "So, Layla," Marcus said, leaning forward on his arms. "What do you do when you're not eating strangers' barbecue?"She smirked. "I'm a medical assistant at Riverside Community Clinic. It's not glamorous, but I like helping people.""That's solid," he said. "I respect folks who do real work.""What about you?" she asked.He hesitated for half a breath. "Construction mostly. Trying to start my own auto-detailing business. Been saving, buying equipment piece by piece."There was pride in his voice, quiet but sure."That's dope," Layla said. "Most people talk about plans like their wishes. You sound like you mean it."He smiled. "I learned the hard way that talking don't build nothing. You just gotta get up and do it."They spent the next hour swapping small stories—childhood summers, favorite foods, the movies they could quote line for line. Layla caught herself laughing until her stomach hurt, the kind of laughter that loosened something inside her chest.When Tasha passed by with a knowing grin, Layla pretended not to notice, but Marcus did. "Your cousin nosey," he said."Always," Layla replied. "She collects gossip like coupons.""She probably already planning our wedding."Layla nearly choked on her drink. "Slow down, we barely know each other."He chuckled. "I didn't say I was proposing. I'm just saying she probably working on a

Pinterest board." They laughed again, the easy kind of laughter that belonged to people who hadn't yet been hurt by each other. As the sun sank lower, the music got louder, the crowd rowdier. Layla found herself leaning against a fence post, paper plate balanced in her hand. Marcus joined her, close enough that she could smell the faint citrus of his cologne beneath the smoke. "Long day?" he asked. "Long week," she said, sighing. "But today was good. Thanks to you—and this sauce." "I told you it was the truth." She smiled, looking down at her food. "Don't get cocky." "I'm humble," he said, mock-serious. "I just happen to be right most of the time." "Is that so?" "Yep." He took a sip of lemonade, watching her over the rim of the cup. "You got a boyfriend, Layla?" The question caught her off guard. She swallowed before answering. "No. Not for a while." "Good," he said. Then, realizing how it sounded, added quickly, "I mean—that's good for you. Time to yourself, I mean." She grinned. "Uh-huh. Sure." By the time people started packing up coolers, the sky had gone from gold to indigo. Cicadas hummed in the trees, and the smell of smoke clung to her hair. Marcus walked beside her toward the curb where her car waited. "You seem like somebody who been through a lot," he said quietly. "Not in a bad way—just... seasoned." "Seasoned?" Layla repeated, laughing. "What am I, a chicken wing?" He laughed too, but then his voice softened. "I mean you move careful. Like you learned what peace costs." That stopped her. She looked up at him, surprised by the weight of his words. "Maybe I have." He nodded slowly. "I respect that. Peace worth protecting." They stood there a moment, the streetlight painting them in pale gold. Layla didn't know what to say, and Marcus didn't seem in a rush for her to. Finally he cleared his throat. "Listen, I ain't perfect. Made some mistakes, learned from 'em. I ain't out here playing games anymore. I just want something real." Layla's heartbeat stumbled at the echo of her own secret prayer. She studied his face—the sincerity in his eyes, the small scar near his temple, the way he didn't look away. "Then start with honesty," she said softly. "Don't tell me what you think I wanna hear." He nodded. "Fair. I can do that." "Good." He smiled, slow and easy. "Then maybe you'll let me prove I'm different." "Maybe," she said, unlocking her car door. "We'll see." Marcus watched her get in, waited until her taillights disappeared down the block. He rubbed a hand over his jaw, the ghost of a smile still tugging at his lips. He hadn't expected her to get under his skin so quick. She wasn't flashy, not loud—but there was something about her steadiness that called to him.Inside her car, Layla gripped the steering wheel, pulse still fluttering. The city lights blurred through the windshield as she whispered to herself, "Don't overthink it. Just breathe."But she was already replaying every line, every glance, every quiet laugh. Something about Marcus felt like possibility. And possibility was something she hadn't let herself feel in a long, long time.She didn't know it yet, but that night was the beginning—the moment the pieces of two tired hearts started shifting toward each other, drawn by something deeper than either could explain.Sometimes love doesn't arrive with fireworks. Sometimes it just shows up with a paper plate, a warm smile, and a promise waiting to be tested.

Chapter 2 – An Unexpected Encounter

The next week crawled by like traffic after a summer thunderstorm. Layla tried to keep her head down at work—charts to file, blood-pressure cuffs to reset, patients to calm—but between every appointment her mind drifted back to the cookout: the smell of smoke in the air, the sound of Marcus's laugh, the way he'd looked right at her as if she were the only person standing in that crowded yard.

The Quiet Between Shifts

Monday morning started with chaos. The waiting room overflowed, the phone wouldn't stop ringing. "Miss Powell, your patient in room 3 ready," the receptionist called.

Layla grabbed the clipboard, pasted on a professional smile, and stepped inside. Even while she worked, fragments of Marcus kept slipping in—the shape of his hands, the rough edge of his voice when he'd said, I just want something real.

By late afternoon, the hallway smelled of disinfectant and burnt coffee. Her friend Janelle nudged her. "You been floating all day, girl. Who is he?"

Layla smirked. "I'm just tired."

"Uh-huh," Janelle teased. "That kind of tired that make you smile for no reason."

Layla rolled her eyes but couldn't hide her grin.

The Text That Changed Her Week

That evening, after dinner and a long bath, Layla sank onto the couch. Her phone buzzed.

Unknown number: Hope your day's treating you right. I still owe you another plate and a real conversation—not one over ribs.

Her pulse quickened. Marcus.

Layla: That sauce was good; I'll give you that. But you confident for a man who almost lost the BBQ challenge.

Marcus: Almost don't count, pretty lady. So, what's your schedule look like this weekend?

After a long pause she typed, Saturday. After five.

Marcus: Say less. I got you.

She laughed softly to herself. You really out here smiling over text messages, huh?

Saturday Preparations

By afternoon the apartment sparkled. Layla had cleaned twice. She checked her reflection, swapped earrings, changed shoes three times.

"You nervous?" Mayah asked, leaning in the doorway.

"Not really," Layla lied.

Mayah grinned. "You been wiping that same counter for twenty minutes. You like him."

Layla sighed. "I like the way he makes me feel … calm."

"That's good," Mayah said. "Just don't forget who you are while you are feeling calm."

Layla smiled. "You turning into Mama."

"Somebody gotta look after you," Mayah said, walking off with a grin.

The Ride

At six sharp, Marcus's silver Altima gleamed at the curb. He stepped out in dark jeans and a white T-shirt, confidence easy as his smile.

He opened her door. "You one of the few men left who still does that," she said.

"Mama drilled it in me. Said if you can't respect a woman, don't talk to her."

Old-school R&B filled the car—Donell Jones, Where I Wanna Be. They drove with the windows cracked, breeze soft, conversation softer.

"You look nice," he said.

"Thank you. You clean up good yourself."

"So, we both winning tonight."

Dinner at the Corner Spot

The soul-food diner sat beside an old record shop, neon sign flickering. Inside smelled like fried catfish and collard greens.

A waitress grinned. "Y'all on a first date, huh? I can always tell."

Marcus laughed. "Guess that means we look good together."

Over plates of baked chicken and cornbread they traded stories—childhood summers, favorite songs, how he wanted to open his own auto-detailing shop. "I want to build something that's mine," he said. "Something nobody can take."

Layla nodded. "Sounds like you've already done a lot of growing."

"Still got a ways to go. Made choices I ain't proud of, but I learned."

"Growth don't happen in comfort," she said.

He smiled at her across the table. "You really different."

"I hear that a lot."

"From men who let you slip away?"

"Something like that," she answered, laughing.

The Drive Home

Later they sat in the car outside her apartment, neither ready to say good night.

"Why me?" she asked quietly. "There were a lot of women at that cookout."

He thought for a moment. "You weren't trying. You were just … peaceful. I noticed that."

"You really pay attention."

"Life got quieter for me after some things I went through. Now I notice what feels real."

He reached over, brushed his thumb across her hand. "I don't wanna move too fast, but I like where this is going."

"Me too," she said.

"Then I'll take my time and do it right."

At her door he hesitated. "Layla, I'm not perfect, but I'm solid. I don't play with hearts."

"Then don't play with mine."

He smiled—slow, sure. "Never that."

When she closed the door behind her, her heart was racing. "Lord," she whispered, "please let this be love, not another lesson."

Outside, Marcus sat behind the wheel, staring through the windshield. For the first time in years, hope didn't feel dangerous. Maybe this time, he thought, he could write a different story.

Chapter 3 – Guarded Hearts

The weeks after their first date settled into an easy rhythm Layla hadn't known she needed.

Morning texts. Evening calls. Little check-ins that told her she wasn't invisible anymore.

Marcus wasn't the kind of man who sent good-morning messages just to keep his name on her screen. He actually listened.

How's Maya doing in school?

You drink water today?

Don't forget to eat lunch, I know you skip it when it's busy.

It was small things—consistent, gentle—that started softening the walls around her heart.

The Routine of Almost Normal

At the clinic, Janelle noticed first.

"Girl, you glowing again," she said one afternoon, shoving a stack of charts toward her. "Whoever this man is, keep him."

Layla laughed. "You acting like I got a fiancé. It's only been a few weeks."

"That's enough for a glow," Janelle said. "Don't ruin it by looking for reasons to be scared."

Layla smiled, but that was exactly what she'd been doing—looking for cracks. Experience had taught her that happiness came with expiration dates. She kept waiting for the moment Marcus would stop calling, stop showing up, stop caring.

But he didn't.

Every evening around the same time her phone would light up:

Marcus: Off work. You eat yet?

Layla: Not really.

Marcus: You know I can't let that slide.

Within an hour he'd be at her door with take-out or groceries. Sometimes they'd cook together in her small kitchen, laughing when the smoke alarm went off. Sometimes they'd eat in silence, just letting the warmth of company fill the spaces where loneliness used to live.

Learning Each Other

One Saturday, Marcus suggested a drive. "I want to show you something," he said.

They ended up at Shelby Farms Park, where the sun was beginning to sink low and turn the lake gold. He pulled a folded blanket and two take-out boxes from the trunk.

"A picnic?" she asked, surprised.

He shrugged. "Ain't gotta be fancy to be special."

They sat beneath an oak tree, the breeze carrying laughter from families in the distance.

After a while she asked, "What made you change? You said before you used to run with the wrong crowd."

He was quiet for a long time. "Losing everything. Freedom. Family. Time. When you sitting in a cell staring at a wall, you start asking yourself what you really worth. God sat me down and made me listen."

Layla studied his face. He wasn't boasting or trying to impress her. He was confessing.

"You regret it?" she asked.

"Every day," he said. "But I also thank God for it. I wouldn't have slowed down long enough to find peace. Or to meet you."

The honesty in his voice reached something deep inside her. For the first time, she wasn't thinking about protecting herself; she was thinking about trusting someone again.

Quiet Growth

Over the next month they became inseparable.

Movie nights. Church on Sundays. Long drives with no destination—just music, conversation, and laughter.

Marcus noticed everything: the way she took her coffee, the gospel song she hummed under her breath, how she always triple-checked that Maya had lunch money.

He'd kiss her forehead and say, "You got a good heart, Lay. Don't let the world make it hard."

One night they sat on her couch with a movie playing quietly in the background.

"You ever think maybe everything you went through was getting you ready for something better?" he asked.

"You mean you?" she teased.

He grinned. "Maybe. Or maybe just the kind of peace you feel when things finally line up."

Layla smiled but didn't answer. Peace was a new language she was still learning.

Shadows Returning

But peace has a way of testing itself.

Late one Thursday, Layla woke to the buzz of Marcus's phone on the nightstand. The screen flashed an unfamiliar number before it went dark again. Marcus stirred beside her, groaned, and reached for it.

"You gonna answer?" she asked softly.

"Nah," he mumbled. "Wrong number."

Something in his tone made her stomach tighten.

The next evening it happened again—another call, another quick excuse.

Finally, she asked, "Everything okay?"

"Yeah," he said too quickly. "Just old friends checking in."

"You sure?"

He forced a smile. "I'm good, Lay. Ain't nothing to worry about."

She nodded, but the unease stayed. She didn't press him—he looked tired, and she remembered his words about the past not letting go easily—but a part of her began to brace itself again, just in case.

The Porch Conversation

A few days later she came home to find him sitting on her porch steps, elbows on his knees, head down.

"Marcus?"

He looked up, eyes heavy. "You ever feel like no matter how far you move forward, the past still right there, pulling on your ankle?"

She sat beside him. "Yeah," she said quietly. "I've felt that."

He rubbed a hand over his face. "Some people I used to run with been trying to reach out. I keep ignoring it, but it's like they smell the peace on me and wanna ruin it."

"Then don't let them," she said. "You've come too far."

He shook his head. "It ain't always that simple.

"Then make it simple," she said, turning toward him. "Choose peace. Choose us."

For a long time, he just stared at her, the streetlight catching the shine of unshed tears.

"You really believe in me like that?"

"I wouldn't be here if I didn't."

He exhaled slowly. "I'm trying, Lay. For real."

She squeezed his hand. "Then keep trying. I'll meet you halfway."

That night, lying awake beside him, Layla stared at the ceiling. She believed in him, but belief came with fear. Love, she realized, wasn't about avoiding pain—it was about having something worth the risk.

And she had found exactly that.

Chapter 4 – Love on Fire

Love has a way of sneaking up quiet, then crashing through every wall you built to keep it out.

For Layla and Marcus, it didn't come with fireworks—it came with consistency, laughter, and the kind of peace neither of them had known in years.

Morning Light

Saturday mornings had become their thing. Layla would wake to the scent of coffee and the low hum of gospel radio drifting from the kitchen. Marcus moved like he belonged there barefoot, humming off-key, making a mess of her spotless counters.

"Morning, sleepyhead," he said as she padded in, still half wrapped in her blanket. He flipped a pancake with a grin. "Hope you hungry."

"You cooking for me again?" she teased.

"Gotta make sure my girl eats right. Can't have you starving for love or breakfast."

She laughed, sitting on the counter. "You're ridiculous."

He leaned close, his voice a low promise. "Yeah, but I'm yours."

He meant it as a joke, but the words hung between them, warm and dangerous. Layla smiled into her coffee, pretending not to blush. "You keep cooking like this, I might start believing you."

Days of Ease

Summer stretched wide and sweet. They'd drive with the windows down, Memphis heat rolling through the car, old-school tracks thumping from the speakers. Sometimes they said nothing for miles, letting the silence be its own kind of comfort.

On lazy afternoons they sat on the porch with iced tea, talking about dreams that felt almost reachable.

Marcus wanted an auto shop— "Not just fixing cars but mentoring young brothers so they don't go where I went."

Layla wanted to finish school, maybe start a small business that mixed healthcare and community outreach.

"You gon' do it," he told her. "You got that fire that don't quit."

"And you?" she asked. "You really think you can pull off that shop?"

He looked out at the street, jaw tight with determination. "I gotta. I'm tired of hustling for other folks' peace while losing mine."

She loved the way he spoke about change—as something he was already doing, not something he only wished for.

The First I-Love-You Almost

One humid evening, rain tapping against the windows, they watched an old movie on her couch. Marcus stretched, resting his hand on her knee. She leaned into him, her head on his shoulder.

He whispered, almost to himself, "I could get used to this."

She smiled. "What, Netflix and take-out?"

"Nah," he said softly. "You. The quiet. The way you make the noise stop."

Her heart stumbled. For a second, she thought he was about to say I love you.

She waited—but he didn't. He just looked at her like the words were there, sitting behind his teeth, not ready to be free yet.

Layla turned her face into his chest, hiding her smile. Maybe they didn't need to say it yet; maybe feeling it was enough.

Little Fights, Big Forgiveness

Real love wasn't perfect, though. They had their moments.

Like the night Marcus came late after promising to pick her up at seven. She'd cooked, lit candles, waited two hours before he finally knocked.

"Car trouble," he explained, breathless, grease still on his hands.

"Phone trouble too?" she snapped.

They argued—sharp words, raised voices. But afterward, he held her while she cried, whispering, "I ain't used to people waiting on me. I'll do better."

And he did. He showed up early next time, flowers in hand, apology still in his eyes.

Layla learned that love wasn't about never falling short—it was about the choice to keep showing up after you did.

Intimacy and Peace

One night the power went out during a storm. Candlelight flickered off the walls, thunder rolled like distant drums.

Marcus traced lazy circles on her arm. "Crazy how quiet feels louder when it's just us," he murmured.

Layla looked up at him, her heart steady for once. "Crazy good or crazy scary?"

"Both."

Their lips met slow, deliberate. The kiss deepened—careful, searching, grateful. When they finally made love, it wasn't rushed. It was communion: two souls that had been scraped raw finally finding somewhere soft to rest.

Afterward, they lay tangled in the dim glow, the storm easing outside.

Layla whispered, "I don't want to lose this."

Marcus pressed a kiss to her forehead. "You won't. I promise."

But promises are only as strong as the world allows them to be.

And the world was about to test theirs.

The weeks that followed were the kind people write songs about.

Sunday mornings, they'd make breakfast together and tease each other about who burned the biscuits. Tuesday nights, he'd show up with groceries and that easy smile that made her forget how hard her day had been. When he wrapped his arms around her, the noise of the world fell away.

But love, Layla was learning, isn't just about peace. It's also about trust—and the fear of what happens when that trust is tested.

A Change in the Air

It started small. Marcus's phone buzzing after midnight. Quick glances at the screen, then the phone flipped face-down.

"You gonna answer?" she asked one night.

"Nah, it's just a buddy from way back."

The answer came too fast. His eyes didn't quite meet hers. Layla didn't push, but she felt a faint chill slide through the warmth they'd built.

The next evening, while they were washing dishes, she tried again.

"You sure everything's okay?"

He dried his hands, leaned on the counter. "Yeah. Just old noise trying to find me again. I told you, I'm done with that."

She reached across the sink and touched his arm. "Then let it stay done."

He nodded, but she could see the tension in his jaw.

Restless Nights

Layla began waking to an empty bed—Marcus sitting outside on the porch, cigarette glowing between his fingers. He said he wasn't smoking anymore, but sometimes you reach for what used to quiet your nerves.

"Can't sleep?" she asked, stepping into the doorway.

"Nah. Just thinking."

"About what?"

He smiled faintly. "About how good it feels to have something worth protecting."

She walked over, sat beside him. The night smelled of rain and asphalt.

"Then protect it," she whispered.

He didn't answer, but he crushed the cigarette out and pulled her close.

Dreams and Detours

A week later, Marcus got a call that made his whole mood shift. He didn't say who it was, just that he needed to handle "some business."

He left early, came home late. Layla tried not to pry but worry sat heavy in her stomach.

When he finally came through the door that night, she was waiting on the couch.

"You can talk to me, you know," she said.

He sighed, dropped onto the cushion beside her. "Remember I told you I owed somebody from before? I'm trying to make that right. Not in a bad way—just closing a door."

"Is it dangerous?"

"No," he said too quickly, then softened. "It's just something I gotta do clean so it don't follow me."

Layla looked at him for a long time. "Then promise me you'll tell me if it gets messy."

"I will," he said. "I don't keep secrets from you."

She wanted to believe that. And for the moment, she chose to.

A Fire and a Prayer

That weekend they drove out past the city limits, found an empty stretch of country road where stars looked close enough to touch. Marcus pulled over, turned the engine off, and leaned back against the hood.

"You ever think about forever?" he asked.

"Sometimes," she said. "Used to scare me. Now it feels like something I could hold."

He smiled. "You the first person who ever made forever sound peaceful."

She reached for his hand, their fingers lacing together under the starlight. "Then let's build it one honest day at a time."

He kissed her then—slow, certain, grateful. And for a while, everything felt safe again.

Foreshadow of the Storm

The next morning, while Layla packed leftovers into the fridge, Marcus's phone lit up again. This time the message preview flashed before the screen dimmed: We need to talk—today.

She froze, staring at the name she didn't recognize. When he walked back in, she smiled like nothing was wrong. But inside, her heart was already tightening, bracing for something she couldn't name.

Because love, no matter how strong, can't always keep the past from knocking.

And the knock was coming soon.

Chapter 5 – The Storm Before the Sentence

The summer heat pressed down heavy, thick enough to taste. The air itself seemed restless—like it knew something was coming.

Marcus felt it first. The unease. The way his phone buzzed more often. The unfamiliar cars parked too long at the corner. He told himself it was paranoia, but the knot in his chest wouldn't loosen.

Layla noticed the shift before he said a word.

He moved different now—eyes always scanning, jaw tight, laughter shorter.

"Talk to me," she said one night while he paced the porch.

He stopped, hands on his head. "Lay … I might need to lay low for a bit."

Her stomach dropped. "Lay low? What does that even mean?"

"It means ... some old folks don't like that I walked away. I ain't done nothing wrong, but they trying to pull me back into mess I outgrew."

"You promised me that life was behind you."

"It is!" he snapped, then caught himself. "I just ... I didn't plan for ghosts to chase me."

Layla folded her arms, voice trembling. "You're scaring me, Marcus."

He stepped closer, softened. "I'd never let nothing happen to you. I just gotta handle this my way."

"Your way got you locked up once."

Silence. Heavy, guilty silence.

"Please," she whispered. "Whatever this is, don't face it alone. Don't let pride be the reason I lose you."

He looked at her like he was memorizing her face. "You already saved me once. Don't worry, Lay. I got this."

Pressure Mounting

Days blurred into each other. Marcus left early, came home late. He smiled, but it never reached his eyes. Layla pretended not to notice; pretending was easier than panicking.

At the clinic, she dropped instruments twice in one morning. Janelle pulled her aside. "Girl, whatever's wrong, fix it before it breaks you."

"I'm fine," Layla lied.

At night she'd lie awake listening for his key in the lock, whispering prayers she hadn't prayed in years.

When he finally came home one Friday, shoulders heavy, she met him at the door.

"Where were you?"

"Talking to a lawyer," he said quietly.

Her pulse stuttered. "A lawyer? For what?"

He exhaled hard. "Some old case they digging up. Stuff from before I met you. I wasn't even there, but they saying I was."

Layla sank onto the couch. "You mean they're … charging you?"

He nodded. "Trying to."

Tears filled her eyes. "Marcus …"

"I'm fighting it," he said quickly. "But if it go bad … I might have to sit down again."

Her breath caught. "How long?"

He looked down. "Could be months. Could be years. I don't know yet."

Layla shook her head. "We were supposed to be building something. You said—"

"I know what I said!" he barked, then covered his face. "I'm sorry. I just … I didn't plan for this, Lay. The past don't care if you changed."

She knelt in front of him, cupped his hands. "Then let's fight it together."

He looked at her, pain swimming behind his eyes. "I don't want you carrying this weight."

"I already am."

He pulled her into his arms, and they stayed like that, both trembling, both pretending they still had control.

The Court Date

The morning of the hearing arrived too soon. Layla ironed his shirt even though he couldn't wear it inside. The courthouse smelled like fear and paperwork.

When the judge read the charge, Marcus stood tall but still. Layla's heart pounded in her throat.

Words blurred together—possession, association, prior record. She clutched her hands until her knuckles went white.

Then the gavel fell.

Two years.

It sounded like thunder cracking open the sky.

Marcus turned toward her, eyes soft but steady, and mouthed, I love you.

The bailiff led him away. The clang of the cell door echoed long after he disappeared.

Aftermath

Layla sat in the car outside the courthouse, staring through the windshield until the rain began to fall. She couldn't even start the engine. All she could hear was that gavel. All she could feel was the weight of a promise breaking in her chest.

At home she folded his hoodie against her chest and whispered, "I got you."

Then, louder, through tears: "I got you, Marcus."

She didn't know how, but she meant it.

Because when love is real, you hold on—even when your hands start shaking.

The first night without him was the longest of Layla's life.

His side of the bed felt cold almost immediately, the silence too big for the room. She left the TV on just to fill the air, but every shadow still looked like him walking through the door.

When the phone finally rang—an unfamiliar number, robotic voice first, "You have a collect call from…"—her heart stopped before it started again.

"Marcus," she breathed into the receiver.

"Hey, baby," his voice came through, rough and hollow under the static. "You okay?"

The question hit her harder than the verdict.

"I'm here," she whispered. "That's all I can say right now. I'm here."

They only had fifteen minutes. He tried to sound strong; she tried not to cry. When the line clicked dead, Layla sat in the dark clutching the phone like it was a lifeline that had slipped from her hands.

The Hollow Days

The world didn't stop just because her heart did. Bills still came. Maya still needed rides and homework help. At work, patients still coughed and complained.

Layla moved through it like a ghost, smiling when she had to, breaking down in the car where no one could see.

Janelle caught her once in the supply closet, eyes red. "You can't pour from empty, girl," she said softly. "You either let the pain eat you or you use it to build something."

Layla wiped her face and nodded. "I'll build."

That night she wrote her first letter.

The First Letter

Hey, love. I don't even know if you'll get this soon, but I need you to hear me. I'm angry. I'm scared. But I'm not leaving. You said you were gonna fight, so I'm fighting too. For us.

She folded the paper carefully, added a photo of the two of them from the cookout—smoke, laughter, sunlight. She sealed it, kissed the envelope, and mailed it the next morning before she could change her mind.

When his reply arrived two weeks later, the handwriting was shaky but steady:

You don't know what your words did for me. Every time I close my eyes, I see you smiling, and that's what's keeping me from losing it in here. Don't give up on me. I'm coming home better than I left.

Layla cried over that letter, then pressed it flat and tucked it inside her Bible. It wasn't just paper—it was proof that love could travel through concrete and steel.

Visiting Hours

The first visit took her breath away. Metal detectors, lockers, the heavy clang of doors. When Marcus walked out in that orange jumpsuit, it was like seeing him through a different lens—still him but dimmed by the place around him.

They sat across from each other at a table bolted to the floor. Guards watched from every corner.

Layla reached for his hands; his fingers trembled when they touched.

"Damn, baby," he whispered. "You really came."

"I told you I would."

His eyes shone. "You the only real thing I got left."

They only had thirty minutes. They filled it with small talk—Maya's grades, his reading list, jokes about prison food—but when the guard called time, she felt like her chest cracked open.

As she stood to leave, Marcus said, "Don't let this place steal your light, Lay."

She squeezed his hands one last time. "Then you don't let it steal yours."

That became their promise.

The Decision to Stay

That night she sat at the kitchen table, pen hovering over blank paper. She thought about walking away—about how easy it would be to stop writing, stop waiting, start over.

But she also thought about every moment they'd shared: the laughter, the honesty, the slow rebuilding of a man trying to be better.

She began to write again, her tears blotting the ink.

I made up my mind. I'm holding it down. Not because I'm weak, not because I don't have options, but because I believe in what we started. I believe in who you're becoming.

When she sealed that letter, she felt something shift inside her. The pain was still there, but underneath it was steel.

The Calm After

Weeks passed. Routine became survival: work, take care of Maya, write letters, pray.

Marcus called whenever he could. Sometimes they laughed. Sometimes they sat in silence, just breathing the same air through the phone.

Love didn't disappear—it evolved. It became endurance, patience, faith. The fire that had once burned bright now glowed steady, a quiet flame that refused to die.

Layla didn't know how long two years would feel, but she knew one thing for sure:

She wasn't counting down the days.

She was building toward them.

Because holding it down wasn't about waiting.

It was about believing.

Chapter 6 – Letters and Lockdowns

The morning after her first visit, Layla woke with puffy eyes and a pounding head. The house was silent except for Maya moving around in her room. For a long time, Layla just stared at the ceiling, wondering how she could miss someone she'd just seen yesterday.

Then she remembered the way Marcus had looked at her through the thick glass—eyes steady, smile tired but still fighting—and she knew why. That look was the reason she would keep showing up.

The First Month

Prison time ran on a different clock. To Marcus, days bled together into a dull loop of roll call, meals, and noise. To Layla, they moved like cold molasses, each sunrise another reminder of the space between them.

She started marking his letters on a calendar: blue ink for his, red for hers. The paper trail grew thicker each week. Some nights she'd fall asleep on the couch surrounded by envelopes, his handwriting curling like a heartbeat across every page.

In her letters she told him about ordinary things—the clinic gossip, Maya's new hairstyle, the sermon from Sunday. She kept the tone light, filling her words with sunlight so he'd feel warmth through the paper. She never mentioned how lonely she was, how she sometimes sat in his hoodie just to breathe him in.

Marcus's World

Inside, Marcus learned quickly that silence was safety. You kept your head down, respected space, watched everything. The first week was rough—too many faces from too many mistakes—but the thought of Layla waiting outside those walls anchored him.

He started attending classes in the prison library, signed up for GED tutoring, and joined a faith circle that met every Wednesday night. In his letters, he wrote:

You'd laugh seeing me with a Bible in one hand and a notebook in the other. But I figure if I want to build a life with you, I gotta learn how to build one right first.

When she read that line, Layla smiled through her tears. He was still trying. That mattered more than anything.

Love by Mail

Every Friday she'd drive to the post office on her lunch break, drop a thick envelope into the slot, and whisper, "Get there safe."

Some weeks she'd include a printed photo—her and Maya at the park, a snapshot of her new haircut, even a picture of the clinic staff goofing around at lunch. Little windows to the world he was missing.

In return, Marcus sent poems. Raw, unpolished, honest. One ended with:

They locked the door, but you still found a way in.

Through ink, through prayer, through everything I used to hide behind.

She pressed that page to her lips before sliding it into her keepsake box. It wasn't about poetry; it was about presence.

Mayah's Adjustment

Mayah asked fewer questions than Layla expected. "He messed up, right?" she said once, sitting on the couch.

"Yeah," Layla admitted. "But he's paying for it. And he's learning."

Mayah nodded. "Then maybe he deserves a second chance. We all do."

Layla blinked back tears. Her little sister had grown up while she wasn't looking.

The Visit Routine

By the second month, visiting day had its own rhythm. Wake early, braid her hair, pack coins for the vending machines. She'd wait through security lines, heart racing until she saw him walk in. Sometimes he'd crack jokes to make her laugh; other days he just held her gaze, memorizing every detail like a starving man storing a meal.

"Time's up!" the guard would bark, and they'd stand slowly, fingers lingering until they had to let go.

Each goodbye hurt, but every visit reminded them why they were enduring. Love didn't live in grand gestures anymore—it lived in thirty-minute windows and paper envelopes.

By the third month, Layla had adjusted to her new normal days that started with work and ended with ink.

Her apartment became half home, half sanctuary. One corner of the dining table was always stacked with envelopes, pens, and printed photos; the other held Maya's schoolbooks and Layla's half-finished coffee cups.

She'd come home from the clinic exhausted, but the moment she opened a letter from Marcus, her body relaxed.

It wasn't just what he said—it was how he said it, careful and steady, as if he were holding her through every line.

Inside the Walls

Marcus wrote about the noise—the way metal doors slammed every hour, the endless chatter and tension. "You gotta stay invisible in here," he said in one letter. "Keep your head down, do your time, and make sure the time don't do you."

But one night, invisibility failed him.

Two inmates started arguing in the chow line, and when one shoved the other, Marcus stepped between them. Instinct, not thought. A guard's whistle cut through the air, and suddenly everyone was shouting.

They sent him to segregation for three days while they sorted it out. In that windowless room, he prayed for patience—and for Layla.

When he finally got back to his cell, he wrote her immediately:

I ain't perfect, baby. Sometimes the old me wanna rise up, but I keep seeing your face. That's what calms me down. You're my peace in a place that don't know the meaning of it.

When Layla read it, she pressed her hand to her heart. "You still mine," she whispered into the empty kitchen. "Still mine."

Faith in the Routine

Sunday mornings became sacred. She'd go to church, sit in the back pew, and pray through the music. Afterwards she'd come home, make tea, and write another letter.

Sometimes Maya joined her, adding a few lines of her own. Hey Marcus, we miss you. Keep doing good things in there.

Layla always smiled when he mentioned those notes in his replies. Tell Maya she my lil' motivator. Tell her she gonna be somebody.

Letters turned into conversations stretched across miles and weeks—confessions of fear, hope, and forgiveness. They prayed for each other through paper.

asked herself why she was waiting.

But every time she thought about letting go, she saw the way he'd looked at her before the

Layla's Quiet Strength

There were nights Layla wanted to quit. Nights when loneliness hit like a wave and she sentencing—like she was the only piece of light left in a dark room.

She kept that memory alive. She turned it into discipline: waking early, cooking real meals, saving money, finishing her degree courses online. "When he comes home," she told Janelle, "he's walking into something stable. I'm not falling apart waiting on him."

Janelle hugged her. "That's love, girl. Not the fairytale kind—the grown kind."

Letters That Healed

Near the end of the year, Marcus's tone changed. His words were lighter, stronger.

They offered me a spot in a mentoring program, he wrote. I'm helping new guys learn trades, how to stay focused. Never thought I'd be the one giving advice, but maybe this what redemption look like.

Layla read that line again and again. Redemption. It felt like a promise. She wrote back, That's who you've always been. The world just had to slow you down long enough to see it.

A Love that Learned to Wait

By the time spring rolled around again, their letters filled two shoeboxes. She tied them with ribbon and kept them under her bed like treasure. Some nights she'd take one out, unfold the pages, and breathe in the faint smell of pencil and disinfectant.

Every word reminded her why she stayed. Every letter proved that love didn't die behind bars—it evolved.

Marcus was learning to forgive himself. Layla was learning that strength didn't always roar; sometimes it wrote quietly in blue ink and refused to fade.

Chapter 7 – Visitation Days

The night before visiting days, Layla could never sleep. No matter how many times she told herself to rest, her mind kept replaying the same questions: Will he look the same? Will he still smile the same? Will he still see me the way he used to?

She laid out her clothes with care—a soft denim skirt, a cream blouse that hid the nervous flutter of her heartbeat. Nothing flashy. Nothing that would get her turned away. Just something that felt like her.

She ironed the fabric twice, spritzed her perfume once, then folded everything neatly on the chair beside the bed.

Tomorrow meant a long drive, a longer wait, and a few short minutes that had to carry her through the next few weeks.

The Drive

Saturday mornings were quiet on the highway. The radio played low—old R&B mixed with gospel—and Maya sometimes rode along, scrolling on her phone while Layla kept both hands steady on the wheel.

Halfway there, the nervousness would start. She'd reach for her cross necklace, rub it between her fingers, and whisper, "Lord, let this visit go smooth."

By the time the prison came into view—tall fences, razor wire glinting in the sun—her throat always tightened. No matter how many visits she'd made, that sight never stopped hurting.

Check-In

Layla had learned the system: ID ready, paperwork filled out, pockets empty. Guards searched her bag, her shoes, sometimes even her hair.

She'd stand quietly, enduring the process with patience she didn't know she possessed.

Other women waited with her—mothers, girlfriends, wives—each one carrying the same mix of fear and devotion. They exchanged polite smiles but few words; everyone understood that pain spoke its own language.

When the doors finally opened, that familiar metallic clang echoed through the hallway like the world shutting behind her.

Face to Face

Marcus always looked different each time she saw him. Some visits he'd appear stronger, his shoulders squared and eyes bright; other days he carried fatigue in the lines of his face.

But the moment their eyes met, everything else faded.

"Hey, beautiful," he'd say, that same half-grin lighting up his whole face.

Layla would smile back, sliding into the hard plastic chair across from him. "You holding up?"

"I'm making it," he'd answer, squeezing her hands across the table. "You look good. You been eating?"

She'd laugh softly. "Trying. You still reading those self-help books?"

He'd grin. "Yeah. But your letters still teach me more."

Each word felt precious, too valuable to waste. They talked about small things—her work schedule, Maya's grades, the sermon from church—but the current beneath every sentence was love and survival.

Moments That Matter

When the vending machine allowed it, she'd buy them chips and sodas, a tiny date in a plastic cup.

Sometimes they shared silence, hands intertwined, communicating through touch more than words.

He'd whisper, "You still my peace," and she'd reply, "Always."

When the guard called, "Time's up," a lump formed in her throat. She'd stand slowly, knowing every second that passed was one less she'd have with him.

He'd lean forward just enough to kiss the air near her cheek, forbidden yet tender.

Walking back through the metal detector, Layla would hold her composure until she reached the car. Then she'd sit behind the wheel, grip the steering wheel tight, and finally let herself cry—quiet tears that never lasted long.

Because she knew he needed her strong.

After the first few months, the visits stopped feeling like events and started feeling like lifelines.

Every other Saturday became sacred—part ritual, part resurrection.

The guard at the front desk even started greeting her by name.

"Morning, Ms. Powell," he'd say, scanning her ID.

Layla would smile politely. "Morning, Officer Davis."

He'd nod toward the waiting area. "He's already on the list. You know the drill."

And she did. She knew every step—the clang of each door, the metallic smell of disinfectant, the buzz that opened the gate to the visitation room.

She knew the sound Marcus's chair made when he stood, the way he rubbed his palms on his pants before reaching for her hands.

The Fellowship of Waiting Women

While waiting, Layla began to notice the other women more.

There was Mrs. Thompson, gray-haired, who came every Sunday to see her son and always brought homemade cookies for the vending machine.

There was Keisha, a young mother with two kids who colored quietly while she talked through the glass.

One morning, Keisha slid into the seat beside her in the lobby. "You been coming a while now," she said. "How you hold it together?"

Layla hesitated. "Prayer. And writing. Every letter I send keeps me sane."

Keisha smiled weakly. "Yeah… that and hope."

They didn't speak again after that, but Layla realized she wasn't the only one holding on to invisible threads of love stretched thin across cold walls.

Marcus's Growth

Each visit revealed something new in Marcus.

The first time she saw him reading, he quoted a line that stuck with her: "Forgiveness is freedom you give yourself."

He told her about the classes he was taking—anger management, vocational training, Bible study.

"I used to think strength was about fighting," he said, eyes lowered. "Now I know it's about walking away when you got something to lose."

Layla smiled, pride swelling in her chest. "That's growth, baby. I see it all over you."

He chuckled. "You sound like my counselor."

"Good," she said. "Maybe that means you listening."

Letters Between Visits

Every visit left her both full and empty. Full of love, empty of time.

So she poured the overflow into letters. Long ones, sometimes ten pages, written late at night under a dim lamp.

You said this place is changing you. Maybe it's changing me too. I'm learning patience I never thought I had. I'm learning that love don't always need touch to stay alive.

When his reply came, the first line read:

You don't know what them words do to me. Every letter from you feels like fresh air through a window that don't open easy.

Those letters became their heartbeat—the rhythm between visits, the pulse of their promise.

The Visit That Broke Her

One Saturday, Marcus looked more tired than usual.

Dark circles framed his eyes; his smile felt forced. Layla knew something was wrong the moment he sat down.

"What happened?" she whispered.

He hesitated. "Lost somebody from the block. A fight broke out last week. He didn't make it."

Layla reached across the table, took his hands, and held them tight. "I'm sorry, Marcus."

He nodded, jaw clenched. "Makes you realize how short this life is. I just… I can't die in here."

Tears burned in her eyes. "Then don't. Keep doing what you're doing. You got people waiting on you."

He looked at her, eyes shining. "You mean you."

She swallowed hard. "Yeah. Me."

For a long moment they just stared at each other, palms pressed together, separated by rules but united by pain.

When the guard called time, Layla stood up but didn't move. She mouthed, I love you.

Marcus mouthed back, I know.

Faith Beyond the Glass

On the drive home, the sunset bled red across the horizon, and gospel played softly through the speakers.

Layla whispered, "Thank you, God, for keeping him another day."

From then on, every visit ended the same way: a quick prayer before leaving the parking lot, asking for protection, patience, and peace.

Back home, she'd light a candle, read one of his old letters, and write a new one before bed.

She knew they still had a long road ahead—but she also knew love had found a way to live inside those walls.

Because every time she saw him walk into that room, she saw not the prisoner, but the man she'd chosen to believe in.

Chapter 8 – Love Through the Phone

The first time the phone rang with that automated voice, Layla's heart nearly stopped.

You have a collect call from… There was a pause, then a familiar breath.

"Marcus," came the low, rough reply.

The system clicked again. Press 5 to accept.

She pressed before the voice finished the sentence.

"Hey, baby."

She didn't mean to cry, but tears came anyway, spilling fast and hot. "I was starting to think you forgot how to dial."

He laughed softly. "Had to wait for the line. Everybody fightin' for the phone in here."

That sound—his laugh—did something to her. It filled every empty space in her apartment.

The New Rhythm

From that day on, her evenings revolved around the phone.

She learned the patterns: the buzz at 7 p.m., the static hum before his voice. Sometimes she'd be cooking dinner or folding laundry when it came; other times she'd sit by the phone ten minutes early, hands trembling.

Those fifteen minutes weren't long, but they were sacred.

"Tell me somethin' good," he'd say.

"I made it through another day."

"That's my girl."

They talked about everything and nothing—about Maya's new boyfriend rumors, the patients who tested Layla's patience, the book Marcus was reading about discipline. The calls became their heartbeat, the steady rhythm of two people determined to keep believing.

The Price of Connection

Each call cost money—too much sometimes—but Layla didn't care.

She budgeted carefully, cut back on small things. She started bringing lunch from home, stopped impulse-buying clothes she didn't need. Every saved dollar meant another call, another moment of his voice saying, "I love you, girl."

Maya noticed the sacrifices. "You don't gotta do all that, Lay."

Layla smiled faintly. "You'd do the same if it was somebody you loved."

Maya nodded, but her eyes said she still didn't understand the kind of love that stretched across bars and bills.

Static and Secrets

Sometimes the calls were clear, filled with laughter and teasing; other times the line cracked, voices fading like ghosts.

"Can you hear me?" she'd ask.

"Yeah… kinda. You sound like you underwater," he'd say, chuckling.

"Maybe that's the Lord reminding you to stay baptized."

He'd burst out laughing, that deep, rich sound she lived for.

But there were nights when silence sat heavy between them.

"Everything okay in there?" she'd ask.

"I'm good. Just... tired."

She knew there were things he couldn't say things the phone lines weren't safe enough to hold.

Still, she listened to the spaces between his words, piecing together the truth by instinct and love.

Unspoken Prayers

One Sunday evening the call came later than usual.

"Hey," he said, voice lower than normal.

"You sound worn out."

"Just been thinking," he admitted. "Sometimes I wonder if this even fair to you."

Her chest tightened. "Don't start that."

"Nah, for real. You could be with somebody free."

She took a breath. "And I'd still be miserable if it wasn't you."

The silence that followed wasn't empty—it was sacred.

"I needed to hear that," he said finally. "You keep me believing."

"Then don't stop fighting," she replied.

Before the line cut off, they prayed together—short, simple words.

God, hold us down until we can hold each other again.

By the third month of calls, Layla could recognize Marcus's tone before he even said a word.

If he started with, "What you doin', pretty lady?" she knew it was going to be a good night.

If he led with a long sigh, she braced herself—something inside those walls was wearing on him again.

Still, no matter what kind of day he had, that phone connected them. It became their world—fifteen minutes carved out of chaos, fifteen minutes where they remembered who they were before orange jumpsuits and glass partitions.

Laughing Through the Distance

One night, the conversation turned silly.

"You still can't cook rice right, can you?" Marcus teased.

"Boy, you in prison and still trying to talk about my cooking?" Layla shot back, laughing.

"Hey, we got rice here too—difference is, ours come with mystery sauce."

"Ew!"

"Yeah," he said, laughing with her. "That's why I'm dreamin' about your home food. First thing I'm eatin' when I get out is your mac and cheese."

Layla smiled, imagining it: him sitting at her kitchen table, sunlight on his face, the smell of baked macaroni and cornbread filling the air.

"Then you better behave in there," she said softly. "So I can make it for you myself."

"Deal," he replied. "You cook, I'll never get in trouble again."

That night they both went to sleep smiling, miles apart but closer than they'd ever been.

The Hard Conversations

Not every call was laughter. Some nights carried the weight of everything they couldn't change.

Marcus told her about men losing hope inside—friends who gave up, families that stopped answering. "Sometimes it feel like time eatin' us alive in here," he said quietly.

Layla's heart twisted. "Then let's starve the time," she said. "We keep writing, talking, praying—whatever it takes."

He didn't respond right away. Then, softly, he said, "You really believe we gon' make it through all this?"

"I don't believe it," she said. "I know it."

The Call That Broke the Rules

Late one night, the phone rang at a time it shouldn't have. Layla froze, staring at the screen. The voice repeated: You have a collect call from…

"Marcus."

She pressed five before logic could stop her.

"Why are you calling this late?" she whispered.

"Had to hear your voice," he said. "Couldn't sleep."

"You'll get in trouble."

"Worth it."

That call was quieter than usual, filled with long pauses and gentle breaths. He talked about the moon he could see through his cell window, how it reminded him of her. "I swear it looks closer tonight," he said.

Layla smiled through her tears. "Maybe that's God letting you know I'm still looking at the same one."

They didn't say "I love you" at the end—it was already understood in the way they breathed each other's names.

Aching Faith

As the months went by, the calls became prayer sessions, therapy, and check-ins all rolled into one.

Some nights he'd quote scripture: "Be still, and know that I am God."

Other times, she'd whisper affirmations into the phone: "You're coming home. You're not your past."

Together, they learned that faith wasn't about ignoring pain—it was about believing through it.

"Every time I hear your voice," Marcus said once, "I remember why I can't give up."

"And every time I hear yours," she replied, "I remember why I still believe in second chances."

When the Line Went Silent

One night the call ended abruptly, the timer cutting off mid-sentence. "I love y—" Click.

Layla sat staring at the phone, waiting for the line to reconnect. It didn't. She knew he'd tried to squeeze in those last seconds, but the machine didn't care about love—it only cared about time.

She whispered into the quiet, "I heard you anyway."

Then she sat back, smiled faintly, and began writing another letter. Because no matter how short the calls were, the love behind them was endless.

The Sound of Hope

Weeks later, Marcus ended a call with something new.

"When I get out, I'm getting my own shop," he said. "A place called 'Second Chance Repairs.'"

Layla's heart leapt. "That's perfect."

He chuckled. "Yeah. Because that's what you gave me—a second chance."

The timer beeped. *You have sixty seconds remaining.*

"Time's almost up," she said softly.

"Then let me say this before it cuts off."

"Say what?"

"That I'm yours," he said, voice steady. "And I ain't ever letting time take that away."

The line clicked, but this time, Layla didn't cry.

She smiled instead. Because faith had finally learned how to sound like love through a wire.

Chapter 9 – The Weight of Waiting

Waiting has a sound.

It's the hum of the refrigerator at midnight, the tick of a clock that seems louder when you're alone.

For Layla, waiting was the echo of Marcus's voice fading through the phone, leaving her in a room full of silence.

Routine Like Armor

By the second year of his sentence, her life had become a schedule of survival.

Up at 6 a.m., coffee, uniform, clinic. She worked double shifts when she could, both for the money and the distraction. Work was predictable; loneliness wasn't.

At night she'd come home, make dinner for Maya, and listen to the same playlist she and Marcus used to ride to. Some nights she'd sing along. Other nights, the lyrics hurt too much to finish.

Janelle noticed. "You ever take a break, girl?"

Layla shrugged. "Can't afford to fall apart."

"Maybe not," Janelle said softly, "but you can afford to breathe."

The Outside Voices

People started talking.

At church, someone whispered, "She still waiting on that man in jail?"

Her aunt called one Sunday: "Baby, I love you, but you wasting your youth."

Layla smiled through gritted teeth. "I'm investing it."

But their words lingered. Late at night she'd lie awake wondering if maybe they were right. What if Marcus got used to being gone? What if the world outgrew the love they'd built?

Then she'd reread his latest letter, see his words—You make me want to be worthy of sunlight again—and the doubt would quiet down.

Marcus's Walls

Inside, Marcus was learning how to survive silence too.

He woke before dawn, did push-ups, wrote in a notebook Layla had sent through a care package. He kept a folded picture of her taped inside the cover.

Sometimes he'd sit on his bunk staring at that photo until his cellmate, Rico, would nudge him.

"Man, you gone burn a hole through that paper."

Marcus smirked. "Only thing keep me from losing it."

Rico chuckled. "You lucky. Most folks in here ain't got nobody waiting."

"Yeah," Marcus said quietly, "I know."

He carried that truth like armor.

The Weight of Letters

Every Friday brought mail call. When the guard shouted his name, the room would quiet. Marcus opened each envelope slowly, careful not to tear her handwriting. Her words smelled faintly of cocoa butter and home.

She wrote about small joys—Maya getting into advanced math, the neighbor's new puppy, the promotion she'd finally earned. Nothing dramatic, just life continuing.

At the end she always added the same line: Still holding it down.

He'd trace those words with his thumb until the ink smudged.

Then he'd write back: You give me something solid to stand on. That's what freedom feels like—even in here.

When Days Blur Together

Weeks passed without incident. Then a fight broke out on the block, and the prison went into lockdown. No calls. No mail. No visits.

For Layla, the silence was brutal. Each day she checked the mailbox like it owed her something. Nothing.

By the tenth day, she was pacing the apartment. Even Maya noticed. "He'll call soon," her sister said. "Don't panic."

Layla forced a smile. "I'm not panicking."

But that night she sat in the dark clutching his last letter, whispering prayers into the stillness.

Inside, Marcus counted days the same way—scratches on notebook pages, prayers whispered under breath. When the lockdown finally lifted, the first thing he did was line up for the phone.

"Lay?"

The sound of her name in his voice broke her open. "I'm here," she said through tears. "Don't ever disappear on me like that again."

"I didn't have a choice," he whispered. "But I swear, I felt you the whole time."

The silence after the lockdown changed something in Layla.

She'd always known waiting was hard—but she hadn't realized how heavy hope could get until she felt the weight of it pressing against her chest every day.

She still smiled at work. Still laughed when Maya cracked jokes. But beneath the surface was exhaustion — the kind that didn't come from work, but from holding on.

Temptations of the Real World

It happened slowly.

A new doctor joined the clinic — tall, charming, polite in that practiced way. Dr. James Whitfield. He smiled too easily and remembered her coffee order by the second week.

"Ms. Powell, you make this place run smoother than any nurse I've worked with," he'd say.

Layla would laugh it off, pretending not to notice the way her heart fluttered — not because she was interested, but because she'd forgotten what simple attention felt like.

One Friday, as they were closing up, he offered to walk her to her car. "You shouldn't be out here alone this late."

"It's Memphis, Doc. I'm good," she joked.

"Maybe," he said, smiling, "but humor me."

They walked in silence until he said softly, "Whoever you're waiting for must be lucky."

She stopped. The words hit like a wave.

"I guess he is," she said finally, her voice steady. "And I am too."

She got in her car before he could respond. The next morning, she mailed Marcus two letters — one about her week, and one about boundaries she refused to cross.

I'm not just waiting on you. I'm waiting with purpose. I want you to know that no one could take your place, even when it's hard.

Inside the Storm

That same week, Marcus faced his own test.

A fight broke out in the yard — old enemies from the past trying to drag him back into the chaos he'd left behind. He walked away once. Twice. The third time, he couldn't.

He didn't swing first, but when it was over, both men were bleeding. The guards dragged them apart. Marcus spent seven days in solitary.

He wrote Layla a letter he wasn't sure would ever reach her.

Baby, I failed this week. I let the old me out. I keep thinking about the look you'd give me if you saw me like that. I'm ashamed, but I want you to know I'm still fighting. Even in the dark.

When the letter arrived, the paper was torn, smudged with something that looked like dirt — or maybe blood.

Layla pressed it to her chest and whispered, "God, keep him steady. Please."

Breaking Down, Building Back

One Sunday morning, Layla didn't make it to church. She stayed home, curled on the couch, unread letters scattered around her.

Maya sat beside her quietly, then said, "He's coming back, you know."

Layla looked up. "You think so?"

"I know so. 'Cause if he's anything like you, he don't quit."

That made her laugh — the kind that hurt and healed at once.

"Maybe you should be the one writing him," Layla said softly.

"I already do," Maya admitted. "Every now and then."

Layla blinked. "You what?"

Maya shrugged. "He's family now. Might as well talk to him like it."

That night, Layla wrote Marcus again. We all waiting on you — not just me. Maya too. So come home right, okay?

Marcus's Night of Surrender

In his bunk, Marcus stared at the ceiling and whispered the prayer he used to hear Layla say.

God, don't let me waste the woman who believed in me.

The noise of the cell block faded until it was just him and that prayer.

He'd made up his mind — no more fights, no shortcuts, no slipping back. If he had to crawl through the rest of his sentence to get to her, he would.

The next morning, he signed up to mentor new inmates in the literacy program. He started reading her letters aloud to younger guys who couldn't read their own mail. Her words became light for more than just him.

The Quiet Victory

Two weeks later, he called.

When she picked up, she didn't even say hello. She just breathed, "You okay?"

"Better," he said. "I made it through."

She smiled through tears. "You always do."

They talked about nothing and everything — the weather, her cooking, the dream he had about them sitting by the water somewhere quiet. By the end of the call, Layla realized something:

She wasn't waiting anymore.

She was enduring.

And there's a difference — waiting is still, endurance is strength in motion.

The Letter That Closed the Distance

The next week, Marcus sent a single page. No poems, no promises — just truth.

I can't give you time back, Lay. But I can give you forever once I'm out. Every second of it.

Layla folded the letter and tucked it into her Bible, right between Psalms and Proverbs. Then she whispered to herself,

"Forever's worth the wait."

Chapter 10 – Prayers and Promises

By the third spring without Marcus, faith became more than a Sunday routine for Layla — it became breath.

Some mornings she woke before the sun, sat at the kitchen table with her coffee and Bible open, whispering the same prayer over and over:

Lord, give me strength to love him right, even from afar. Give him strength to find himself in You.

She didn't always feel holy; sometimes she felt angry, tired, or numb. But prayer wasn't about perfection anymore — it was about surviving.

The Church on Madison Street

One rainy Sunday, she almost skipped service. But something told her to go.

The choir was already singing when she slipped into her usual back pew. "I'm still here… by the grace of God." The lyrics hit too close.

Halfway through, the pastor started preaching about restoration — how broken things could still be rebuilt stronger.

Layla felt something stir inside her. When the altar call came, she stood without thinking, tears streaming as she whispered, "Fix me, Lord. Fix us."

Afterward, an older woman touched her arm. "Baby, whatever it is, keep praying over it. God don't waste pain."

Layla nodded. "Thank you." She didn't tell the woman she was praying over a man behind bars — some things didn't need explaining.

Marcus's Turn Toward Faith

Inside, Marcus was sitting on a metal chair in the chapel. The prison chaplain, an ex-Marine with a calm voice, read from Romans:

"Be transformed by the renewing of your mind."

Marcus couldn't stop thinking about that line. Renewing. Maybe that's what he'd been doing all along — renewing piece by piece.

After the service, he stayed behind. "Chaplain, you think people like me can really change?"

The man smiled. "Only ones who don't change are the ones who quit trying."

That night Marcus knelt by his bunk for the first time in years.

He didn't ask for early release. He didn't ask for favors. He just said, "Thank You for not letting her give up on me. Help me be worthy of the woman who waited."

Letters of Light

Their letters began to sound different.

Marcus wrote less about surviving and more about becoming. He told her about teaching literacy classes, about the young inmate who reminded him of himself.

Layla wrote about the kids at church calling her "Miss Lay," about learning how forgiveness could feel like freedom.

In one letter, Marcus wrote:

I used to pray for doors to open. Now I just pray to walk right when they do.

She wrote back:

That's what growth looks like — not getting out, but moving different when you do.

The Phone Call of Peace

A few weeks later, his voice over the line sounded lighter.

"You sound different," Layla said.

"I feel different," he answered. "It's like I stopped fightin' the time and started usin' it."

"That's what I been praying for."

He laughed softly. "Guess God really do hear you."

The timer beeped, warning the call was almost over.

"Before it cuts," he said quickly, "thank you for believing in me before I did."

"You gave me something to believe in," she whispered back.

Click.

She sat staring at the phone, smiling through tears. For the first time in a long while, the silence afterward felt peaceful.

This half brings Layla and Marcus to a place of clarity and commitment, as they turn faith into action and begin planning for their future beyond prison walls.

You can paste it right after Part 1 in your Word manuscript.

The more they prayed, the closer they grew — not just to each other, but to something bigger.

Love was no longer just romance; it was restoration. It was discipline. It was faith with skin on it.

The Journal of Promises

Layla started a new journal. The first page read "When He Comes Home."

Each night, she wrote a promise.

Promise #1: I won't make the past a prison we live in.

Promise #2: I'll never stop praying, even when everything looks fine.

Promise #3: I'll build a life that already feels like peace before he returns.

Some nights, she left the journal open by the window, whispering, "Let these words find him somehow."

Marcus's Notebook

Inside, Marcus was doing the same thing — though he didn't know she was.

He'd gotten a small composition book from the commissary and started filling it with verses, goals, and reflections.

The first page read: "Freedom starts before the gate."

He wrote about wanting to open his auto shop, to speak to young men about avoiding the traps he fell into.

But most of all, he wrote about Layla — how her letters made him feel like a man again, not just an inmate.

You remind me that I'm more than my mistakes. You teach me to see myself through God's mercy instead of my shame.

When the chaplain saw him writing, he smiled. "That right there? That's the beginning of redemption."

Shared Scriptures, Shared Healing

They started reading the same Bible passages — Layla on the outside, Marcus on the inside.

Psalm 40 became their shared anchor: "He lifted me out of the pit, out of the mud and mire; he set my feet on a rock."

One Sunday evening, their phone call turned into a devotion.

"You got your Bible with you?" she asked.

"Always," he said.

"Read Psalm 40."

He read slowly, his deep voice steady. When he finished, she said quietly, "That's us. Pulled out of the mud."

He smiled. "And planted on solid ground."

Layla's Growth

Outside those walls, Layla was changing too. She started volunteering at the community center, helping women write resumes and finish GED applications.

Each time someone thanked her, she thought of Marcus — of the way brokenness could still bloom into something useful.

Janelle noticed the difference. "You glowing again," she said one afternoon.

Layla laughed. "Maybe it's peace."

"Maybe it's love with direction," Janelle replied.

That night, Layla added another line to her journal: Promise #4: I'll never let fear convince me love was a mistake.

A Test of Trust

One evening, Marcus called sounding tense. "Lay, they moving me to another unit."

Her heart jumped. "Why?"

"Overcrowding. I'll still get mail, but visits might be harder for a while."

She exhaled slowly. "We'll adjust."

He paused. "You sure?"

"I've come this far, haven't I?" she said, half laughing, half crying.

He chuckled softly. "Yeah… You built for this."

"Both of us are," she said.

That night, she prayed harder than she had in months. Not out of fear, but out of gratitude — because even through separation, their faith had become unbreakable.

Written Vows

Weeks later, Marcus sent a letter longer than any he'd written before. At the end were words she'd never forget:

This ain't just waiting anymore. This is covenant. When I walk out those gates, I'm not coming home to start over. I'm coming home to finish what we began — a love that didn't die, it just learned how to breathe through walls.

Layla folded the letter slowly, pressing it against her heart. Then she opened her journal and wrote her final promise:

Promise #5: When he returns, I'll meet him not as the woman who waited — but as the woman who grew.

She whispered into the quiet, "Amen."

Chapter 11 – Time Keeps Moving

Time had a strange way of softening everything. The ache of separation, the sting of old memories — none of it disappeared, but it started to hurt less sharply.

Layla no longer counted days; she counted *progress*.

Every sunrise meant she was one day stronger, one day closer to the life they were rebuilding — even if it was happening one letter, one prayer, one heartbeat at a time.

A New Season Outside

Spring melted into summer, and life began to bloom again around Layla. Maya turned seventeen, started talking about college. The clinic promoted Layla to senior medical assistant, and her supervisor mentioned a nursing scholarship. She smiled humbly, pretending she wasn't shaking inside at the idea of going back to school.

That evening she wrote Marcus about it. *They offered to pay for me to go back for my RN license. I'm scared, but maybe this is what faith looks like — moving even when you don't know what's waiting on the other side.*

Two weeks later, his reply came.

Baby, you don't see it, but you already walking in purpose. You Ain't just holding me down — you rising. Go get that degree. I need to come home to a boss.

Layla laughed reading it, but tears welled up anyway. For the first time, she realized that even though Marcus was locked up, he still found ways to push her forward.

The Growth Inside

Marcus's world had changed too. The once-quiet man who kept his head down had become something else — a mentor, a teacher, a leader. He spent his mornings tutoring other inmates, helping them write letters home or study for the GED exam. The chaplain called him "steady hands." The younger guys called him "OG."

Sometimes he still woke up haunted by the past — the mistakes, the lost years — but he didn't stay stuck there anymore. When Rico got into another fight, Marcus pulled him aside. "Anger don't make you strong, bro.

It just makes you tired." Rico laughed bitterly. "What, you a preacher now?" "Nah," Marcus said, smiling faintly. "Just a man who learned the hard way."

That night, he wrote Layla about it.

Every time I stop somebody else from making the same dumb move I did, I feel like I'm paying the world back a little. She kept that letter folded in her wallet — a reminder that love could create change even behind bars.

The Rhythm of Waiting

By year four, the waiting didn't hurt the same. It just *was*. Layla had her routines — work, school, visits, letters. The pain had turned into purpose. Even the other women at visitation started noticing.

"You always so calm," Keisha said one morning. "How you do it?" Layla smiled. "I stopped fighting time. I started living inside it." Keisha laughed. "That sound deep." Layla grinned. "It's survival." And maybe it was. Because love wasn't about the rush anymore — it was about endurance, faith, and the quiet kind of joy that came from knowing she was exactly where she was meant to be.

A Glimpse of Tomorrow

One Friday, Marcus's call came with a new tone — cautious, hopeful. "They reviewing some old cases," he said. "My counselor said I might be up for early release." Layla froze. "Wait… what?" "Don't get too excited yet. Could be months. Could be longer. But it's something." She couldn't stop smiling. "That's *everything, Marcus.*" "I ain't say nothin' definite," he said, laughing. "Don't go pickin' out curtains yet." Layla laughed too, but her heart whispered, *Soon.* That night she didn't write a letter. She wrote a prayer. *God, if this is the start of freedom, let it be real. Let him walk out different. Whole. Ready.* Hope can be heavy when you've carried pain too long. For Layla, the thought of Marcus possibly coming home made her heart race — but it also scared her. She'd built her strength around waiting. What would she be when the waiting was over?

The False Start

Two months later, Marcus called with a tremor in his voice. "Lay, you sittin' down?" "Yeah," she said quickly, gripping the phone tighter. "They denied it." She went silent. "They said my record's clean, progress noted… but they still want me to finish the full sentence." Her throat tightened. "After all that work? After everything you done to change?" "Yeah. Guess God ain't done teachin' me yet." She wanted to cry, to curse, to scream — but she didn't. Instead, she said softly, "Then we keep going." There was a pause. Then he whispered, "You still in this with me?" "Marcus, I was in it before they locked you up. I'll be here when they unlock you too." The call ended with quiet breathing, no words left to give. But the silence felt like agreement. They were both still standing.

The Days After

The disappointment settled into the house like dust. Even Maya felt it. "You okay?" she asked one night. Layla nodded. "Yeah, baby. Just… tired." "You think he's okay?" Layla smiled faintly. "He will be. He's stronger than he used to be." She didn't say the part she was too afraid to speak aloud — that sometimes, faith felt like carrying a cross no one else could see.

Marcus's Darkness

Inside, Marcus spent three days barely speaking. The news hit harder than he expected. Freedom had felt so close he could taste it, and now it was gone again.

Rico found him sitting on his bunk, staring at the wall. "Man, you actin' like it's over," Rico said. "Feels like it," Marcus muttered. Rico shook his head. "You the one always preachin' about patience and purpose. Don't quit now." Marcus cracked a small smile. "Guess I needed to hear my own sermon." That night, he opened his Bible again — Psalm 27 this time. *"I remain confident of this: I will see the goodness of the Lord in the land of the living."* **He read it three times, then whispered, "Layla, I'm comin' home. Maybe not soon, but right."**

Letters That Strengthened

The next week, he wrote her a letter longer than any before. I ain't gonna lie — I broke down when they told me no. But then I thought about you. How you kept movin', kept livin', even when life told you to quit. You

taught me how to keep goin'. So that's what I'm doin'.
Layla read that letter twice, tears falling onto the paper.
Then she wrote back: We ain't waiting anymore, Marcus.
We're preparing. That's a different kind of faith.

Finding Joy in the Middle

After that, time didn't feel like a punishment anymore. It felt like training. Marcus doubled down on his classes and volunteered to lead group sessions. Layla finished her nursing prerequisites, her GPA strong enough to qualify for the scholarship. When they talked on the phone, their laughter came easier again. "You know you gon' be Nurse Powell when I get out?" She smiled. "And you gon' be Mr. Second Chance Repairs." He laughed. "Sound like a power couple to me." "More like a miracle couple," she said, grinning. He chuckled. "Either way, we blessed."

The Last Page of the Year

As the holidays came around, Layla decorated the apartment with Maya — twinkle lights, cinnamon candles, the smell of cookies in the oven. She mailed Marcus a card that read, *Love don't pause for time.* Inside, he hung it on the wall above his bunk, right beside her photo. When the clock struck midnight on New Year's, he whispered to himself, "This the last year I spend in here. I can feel it." And though she couldn't hear him, Layla whispered the same thing across miles and steel: "This is the year you come home."

Chapter 12 – The Unexpected News

The envelope looked ordinary—white, slightly creased, her name written in neat cursive. It was the handwriting that stopped her: Mrs. Henderson, Marcus's mother. Layla's hands shook as she opened it at the kitchen table, the smell of coffee and rain hanging in the air.

> *"Sweetheart, I wanted to tell you before Marcus hears. I've been sick for a while now. They say it's stage two. I'm keeping my faith, but I need you to help me keep his. Don't let him fall apart when he finds out."* The letter ended with, *"You've already*

become family. Thank you for loving my son when the world couldn't." Layla sat there frozen, tears sliding silently down her cheeks. The paper blurred until she couldn't read it anymore. Maya's voice drifted from the hallway, "Lay? You okay?" Layla folded the letter carefully. "Yeah, baby. I'm just … praying."

Telling Him Without Breaking Him

That night she sat down to write Marcus, starting and stopping a dozen times. How do you tell someone trapped behind concrete that the woman who raised him is sick—and he can't even hold her hand?

She finally wrote:

Baby, there's something I need to tell you, and I'm saying it with love and faith. Your mom's been diagnosed, but she's strong. She asked me to tell you myself because she didn't want you worrying. She's in treatment, surrounded by prayer. We're all believing for healing. She sealed the envelope, kissed it, and whispered, "God, carry this letter gentle." For the next ten days she waited. Every hour felt like a test. When the phone finally rang, her knees nearly gave out. "Lay," Marcus said, voice thin. "I got your letter." Her throat tightened. "I'm here." He breathed heavy through the static. "Why she ain't tell me herself?" "She didn't want you to hurt." He was quiet for a long moment. Then, softly: "You think she gon' be okay?" "I believe she will," Layla said, tears already falling. "And we're gonna believe together."

Between Two Prayers

Marcus called again the next evening, calmer. "Lay, you talk to her lately?" "Yesterday. She sounded strong. Said she been eating again." He exhaled. "That's good." He went silent,

then whispered, "You know, she the reason I learned to pray when I was a kid. I used to laugh

at her, talkin' to God like He was sittin' on the porch. Now I get it." Layla smiled through her tears. "Maybe that's what faith really is—still talking like He right there, even when you can't see Him." They stayed on the phone until the timer cut them off. Afterward, Layla knelt by her bed and whispered,

"Lord, if you're sitting anywhere near that porch, please listen."

Letters That Held the Weight

Over the next month, letters between them carried more prayer than conversation.

Marcus wrote:

> *I ain't asking for a miracle for me, but for her. She gave me everything when I had nothing. I just need to see her again outside these walls.*

Layla replied:

> *You will. God don't start stories He don't plan to finish.*

She started visiting Mrs. Henderson every other weekend. They'd sit in the living-room with gospel playing low while Layla filed insurance papers and kept her company through chemo fatigue.

"Marcus always said you had a calming spirit," the older woman murmured one afternoon.

Layla smiled gently. "He got that same spirit in him. Just buried under time. "Then you keep digging, baby," she said. "'Cause that boy gon' need it when he gets out.". The news changed something inside Marcus.

He started waking up before the lights came on, staring at the ceiling while memories of his mother played like old film reels—her laughter while cooking Sunday dinners, her voice calling him "my stubborn boy," the way her hugs made the world quiet.

He couldn't shake the guilt.

"I wasn't there," he whispered one morning to his bunkmate, eyes distant. "All she got left is phone calls and prayer."

The man beside him, an older inmate named Lenny, said softly, "Then make them phone calls count.

Sometimes all folks need to hear is your voice reminding them they still matter." Marcus nodded, but the ache didn't ease.

The Call That Healed

That weekend, Layla arranged a three-way call between him and his mother. She'd spent all morning on hold, talking to the prison staff and the nursing center, just to make it happen. When his mother's voice came through, shaky but alive, Marcus froze. "Ma?" "Baby…". He swallowed hard. "You sound tired."

"I'm all right," she said. "Got good days and some slow ones. But hearing you—Lord, it's good to hear you."

Tears rolled silently down Layla's cheeks as she listened. She didn't speak, just let them have their moment. "I'm sorry I ain't been there," Marcus said. "I should've been a better son." His mother laughed softly. "You still my boy. And you *are* here. Every letter, every prayer—don't think I don't feel it." "Ma, I'm gon' do right when I get out. I promise."

"I already know that" she said. "Cause you got a woman beside you who love you through your mess. That's proof God still got His hand on you."

Marcus closed his eyes, letting the words soak through years of regret.

"I love you, Ma." "I love you more."

When the call ended, the silence afterward was thick with peace.

Layla's Quiet Burden

That night, Layla drove home from the nursing center under a low orange sunset.

Her chest felt heavy but whole.

She'd spent the day helping Mrs. Henderson sort through old photos—Marcus as a boy, gap-toothed and grinning beside a beat-up bicycle.

"Keep this one," the older woman had said, pressing the photo into Layla's palm. "Give it back to him when he come home. I want him to remember who he was before the world tried to break him."

Now, alone in her car, Layla clutched that photo like a promise.

She whispered, "He's coming home, I swear it."

Inside, the Fire Rekindled

Marcus threw himself back into the faith group with new focus. He organized prayer circles, started journaling, and even wrote a testimony the chaplain asked him to share.

In it, he wrote:

> *Sometimes love come through letters. Sometimes through silence. But the strongest love is the kind that show up when you too far gone to fix it yourself.*

> The day he read it aloud, a hush fell over the chapel. Afterward, one of the younger inmates came up and said, "You talk like you already free."

> Marcus smiled faintly. "Guess that's the goal, right?"

The Hospital Visit

A few weeks later, Layla got a late-night call. Mrs. Henderson had been admitted again.

She drove straight to the hospital, hair tied up, heart pounding.

When she walked into the room, the older woman smiled weakly.

"You came quick."

"I told you, I got you."

They prayed together. When the nurses dimmed the lights, Mrs. Henderson whispered, "If I don't make it, tell my boy he already made me proud. Tell him that's enough."

Layla's tears fell onto the woman's hand. "You'll tell him yourself."

The Letter That Changed Him

Marcus got Layla's next letter a week later. Inside was his mother's message written in her handwriting:

Son, I'm tired but grateful. You don't owe me nothin'. Just live right. That's all the payback I need.

He read it three times, then folded it carefully and tucked it into his Bible.

When he called Layla that night, his voice was rough but steady.

"She gon' be okay," he said, almost convincing himself.

"She's resting," Layla said softly. "And she's proud."

They didn't say "goodbye" before the timer cut off that night. They just said "I love you" over and over until the line went dead.

A New Kind of Strength

Weeks passed. Mrs. Henderson's health stabilized, and Marcus began to smile again.

Layla noticed it in his letters — more hope, more gratitude, more peace.

In one letter, he wrote:

I used to ask God why He kept breaking me. Now I realize He was rebuilding me instead.

Layla tucked that one beside the photo in her nightstand. Both reminders of what love looked like when it refused to quit.

Chapter 13 – Breaking Points

There comes a time when even the strongest heart starts to shake.

Layla had spent years being solid — the one who prayed, wrote, showed up.

But strength, she was learning, didn't mean never breaking. It just meant learning how to keep moving while you did.

The cracks showed quietly at first.

Missed meals. Sleepless nights. A laugh that didn't sound like hers anymore.

By early autumn, her days felt like reruns — work, home, study, silence.

Even Maya started noticing.

"You okay, Lay?" she asked one night, leaning against the doorframe.

Layla forced a smile. "Just tired."

"You been tired for months," Maya said softly. "You need to take care of you too."

Layla brushed her off, but the words stuck.

The Routine of Missing Someone

Every evening she sat by the window with her phone, waiting for his call.

When it didn't come, she told herself he was busy — helping in the chapel, writing letters, mentoring the younger guys.

But sometimes, she'd stare at that silent screen and whisper, "Why do I feel more alone now than I did before?"

The next call came two days late.

"Hey, beautiful," Marcus said, his voice warm but strained.

She hesitated. "Hey."

"You sound off. Everything okay?"

"Yeah, just… long week."

She wanted to say more but didn't. Didn't want to make him feel guilty for not being there.

He talked about his classes, his plans, his progress. She listened, but part of her mind drifted — to unpaid bills, to empty space beside her in bed, to how hard it was to hold on to hope when the world kept moving without them.

When the call ended, she whispered to the empty room, "I'm doing everything right, God. So why does it still hurt this much?"

The Night It Cracked

One evening after work, she came home to find a final notice taped to her door — the electric bill.

Her hands shook as she sat on the couch, surrounded by unopened envelopes, exhaustion pressing like a weight on her chest.

Her phone buzzed — Marcus calling.

She stared at it, then let it ring out.

It wasn't anger. It was emptiness. She didn't have the energy to be strong tonight.

A text came through moments later: *"You good?"*

She typed, *"I'm fine,"* then deleted it.

Instead, she wrote, *"Just tired."*

Then turned off her phone.

That night, for the first time in years, she didn't write him a letter.

Marcus Feels the Shift

Inside, Marcus could sense something changing.

When her letters stopped, he checked the mail twice a day. Nothing.

He told himself she was busy, maybe sick, maybe overwhelmed. But deep down, he knew. He'd felt this distance before — that slow fading that came when the world outside got too heavy.

He asked the chaplain for advice.

"She's tired," the man said. "You can't blame her. Loving through distance is the hardest kind of faith."

"So what do I do?"

"You remind her that she's not doing it alone."

That night, Marcus wrote a letter longer than any before.

> *Lay, I know it's getting heavy. I can feel it through the silence. But you ain't by yourself. You never were. Every prayer you said for me — I been saying back for you.*

He folded it carefully, sealing it like it was made of glass. "Get to her," he whispered before sliding it into the outgoing box.

When the Letter Arrived

Three days later, Layla found the envelope in her mailbox — his handwriting, neat and familiar.

She opened it on the porch, sunlight falling over her lap as she read.

> *I can't give you my arms right now, but you still got my heart. Don't let the world convince you you're fighting alone. You holding me down, but I'm holding you too — from here.*

Tears spilled fast, hot, relentless. For the first time in weeks, she let herself feel everything — anger, exhaustion, love, and gratitude tangled into one.

She pressed the letter to her chest and whispered, "Okay. I'm not done yet."

The night air was thick and restless, thunder rumbling somewhere far off.

Layla sat on her couch with Marcus's letter in her lap, the words looping in her mind.

You holding me down, but I'm holding you too — from here.

Her phone rang.

For a second, she thought about letting it ring again. But this time, she couldn't.

She answered.

"Hey," she said softly.

"Hey, beautiful," Marcus replied, his voice warm, almost relieved. "Been missing you."

Layla swallowed. "I know. I just… needed a minute."

There was silence. Then he said, "I get it. But talk to me, Lay. Don't shut me out. That's the only way we make it through this."

Her voice cracked. "You don't get it, Marcus. You still have structure — a schedule, people around you, time to think. Out here, it's just me and bills and loneliness and everyone asking why I'm still waiting for a man who ain't even home yet."

He went quiet. The sound of her crying filled the line.

"I'm trying so hard," she whispered. "But sometimes I feel like I'm carrying us both."

Marcus closed his eyes, breathing through the ache in his chest.

"I know you are," he said finally. "And I hate that I put you in this position. I hate that you gotta be both strong and soft at the same time."

"Then why does it still feel like I'm losing?"

"You ain't losing, baby," he said gently. "You surviving. You doing what love really is — showing up even when it don't feel good."

She exhaled shakily. "But what if one day I can't?"

He didn't answer right away. Then, softly, "Then I'll hold on for both of us. Just like you did for me."

The Honesty They Needed

"Marcus," she said, voice steadier now, "sometimes I wish I could just wake up and not love you this much. It'd be easier."

He gave a tired laugh. "Trust me, I know. But I don't want easy no more. Easy got me here. I want real — even when it's hard."

She nodded, wiping her eyes. "You really mean that?"

"Yeah. I ain't got nothin' left to lie for. You my truth now."

The timer beeped — five minutes left. The sound made both of their hearts clench.

"Listen," Marcus said, "I ain't gon' promise I'll never mess up again, or that I won't get tired, too. But I can promise I'll never stop trying for you. You hear me?"

"I hear you."

"Say it back."

She smiled faintly through tears. "I'll never stop trying for you either."

The Aftermath of Honesty

When the call ended, Layla didn't cry this time. She just sat still, breathing. The room felt lighter — like finally, the truth had opened a window.

She looked at Marcus's letter again, now tear-stained and folded at the corners.

Then she took out her own notepad and began to write.

Marcus,

You're right — love isn't easy. But maybe it's not supposed to be. Maybe it's supposed to stretch us, strip us, rebuild us until we both become the kind of people who can handle it.

I don't know what tomorrow looks like, but I still choose you.

When she sealed the envelope, she smiled for the first time in weeks.

Inside, Marcus received that letter three days later. He read it twice, folded it carefully, and tucked it inside his Bible beside his mother's message. He whispered, "She still choosing me."

And for the first time in months, he slept through the night.

Love's Quiet Recovery

The days that followed were gentler.

Their phone calls turned softer — not rushed, not forced. Just two people learning how to breathe together again through distance.

Layla went back to her routines, but with a lighter spirit.

Maya noticed it one evening. "You smiling again," she said.

Layla laughed quietly. "Guess I remembered why I started waiting in the first place."

Marcus wrote her that week:

> *You showed me that breaking ain't the same as quitting. Sometimes God gotta crack what's solid to make room for something stronger.*

She read that line over and over, whispering to herself,

"Then we must be unbreakable."

Chapter 14 – The Confession

The air in the visitation room buzzed with quiet noise — low chatter, guards' footsteps, the metallic hum of keys and locks.

Layla sat at the far table, her palms pressed flat against the cool surface, nerves prickling beneath her skin.

Marcus walked in a few minutes later, his posture straighter than usual, but his face unreadable.

When their eyes met, her chest eased for a moment — until she saw the weight behind his smile.

Something was off.

He sat down across from her, hands clasped, and for the first time in a long while, he didn't reach for hers.

"What's wrong?" she asked softly.

He exhaled slowly. "There's something I need to tell you, Lay."

Her heart skipped. "Okay…"

He looked down, jaw tight. "It's about before I got locked up. Something I never told you — not 'cause I wanted to lie, but 'cause I wasn't ready to face it myself."

Layla leaned forward, bracing herself. "Go on."

The Truth Comes Out

Marcus rubbed the back of his neck. "Remember how I told you they charged me for being part of that job, but I wasn't there that night?"

"Yeah."

His eyes flickered. "I wasn't there — but I *knew* about it. And I ain't stop it."

The words hit the air like a drop of water in oil — quiet, but explosive.

Layla stared at him, her voice barely above a whisper. "You knew?"

"Yeah."

"And you didn't say anything?"

He shook his head. "I told myself it wasn't my business. I just wanted out. But when it all went bad, somebody got hurt. Not killed — thank God — but hurt bad. I wasn't there, but I might as well have been. My silence made me guilty too."

Layla's heart thudded hard against her ribs.

She couldn't speak for a moment. Her mind was a storm — shock, anger, hurt, confusion, all crashing together.

Marcus kept talking, voice low, almost trembling.

"I been carrying that for years. Thought time would bury it. But every time you looked at me like I was better than my past, I felt like a fraud. I ain't the man you think I am, Lay."

The Silence Between Them

Layla looked at him — really looked. The man who made her laugh, who wrote her poetry on scrap paper, who prayed with her over the phone — now confessing the ugliest part of his story.

Her eyes filled, but her voice stayed calm. "Why now?"

"'Cause I don't wanna walk out of here still half-truth," he said. "You deserve all of me — even the parts I hate."

She nodded slowly, fighting the sting of betrayal and the ache of compassion.

"I asked you for honesty," she said quietly. "And you gave it. But that don't mean it's easy to hear."

"I know."

She looked down, fingers twisting her bracelet. "I just… I built my peace around believing you were innocent. And now I don't know where to put this."

Marcus's eyes softened. "Then put it where grace lives. That's where I been tryin' to stay."

The timer announced the last five minutes. Neither moved. The silence felt like a prayer that couldn't find words.

When the guard finally called time, Layla stood slowly. "I need to think."

He nodded. "I'll wait."

And for the first time since they'd met, she walked away without looking back.

The drive home was a blur.

Rain hit the windshield in thick, uneven streaks, matching the rhythm of her heartbeat. Layla barely remembered the turns she took or the traffic lights she stopped at. All she could hear was his voice echoing in her mind — *"I knew about it."* By the time she parked outside her building, the rain had turned into a full storm. She sat there in the driver's seat, gripping the steering wheel, eyes burning.

"God… why now?" she whispered. "Why after everything we been through?"

She didn't cry right away. The tears came slow, stubborn — the kind that build behind your eyes until they finally break loose.

The Weight of Truth

Inside, she curled up on the couch, still wearing her coat. The room was dark except for the streetlight flickering outside.

She wasn't angry because he'd done wrong — she already knew he'd made mistakes. She was angry because he'd *hidden* one.

All those nights she'd prayed for his peace, she hadn't known he was still carrying a secret too heavy to speak.

She thought of his words: *You deserve all of me — even the parts I hate.*

And somehow, that was what hurt and healed at the same time.

By morning, exhaustion replaced fury. She got up, showered, and went to work like nothing had happened — like her world hadn't shifted overnight.

But that night, when she sat at the kitchen table with pen and paper, her hand froze over the page.

She didn't know what to write.

The Letter She Didn't Send

She tried, over and over, crumpling sheets of paper until they covered the table.

I still love you, but I don't know how to trust you right now.

I wish you'd told me sooner.

You're not the man I thought you were — but maybe that's the point.

Each draft felt half-true, incomplete.

In the end, she tore them all up and whispered, "Not yet."

Instead, she prayed. Not the calm, churchy kind of prayer. The kind that sounded more like a cry.

"Lord, if You put me in this man's life for a reason, show me what to do with the truth he just gave me. Don't let me harden, but don't let me be blind either."

Marcus's Waiting

Back inside the facility, Marcus hadn't slept in two days.

He replayed her face — the shock, the hurt, the quiet strength in her eyes. He'd prepared himself for anger, maybe even rejection, but the silence afterward scared him more than anything.

Rico noticed. "You look like you lost your best friend, man."

Marcus gave a hollow laugh. "Maybe I did."

The chaplain found him in the chapel later that week.

"You did right, telling her," He said.

"Then why it feels like I just killed something?"

"Because truth always costs. But it's the only thing that buys freedom."

Marcus nodded slowly, staring at the tiny cross on the wall. "Then I hope she knows that's all I wanted — to be free with her, not from her."

The Return

A week later, Layla finally walked back into visitation.

Marcus was already sitting there, eyes rimmed red from lack of sleep. When she walked in, his breath caught.

She sat down across from him, silent for a long moment.

Then she said quietly, "You hurt me."

He nodded. "I know."

"You had all this time to tell me, and you waited until now."

"I was scared," he said. "Scared you'd stop seeing me as more than my past."

"I didn't fall in love with a lie, Marcus," she said, voice trembling. "But I did fall in love with a man who didn't trust me with the whole truth."

He looked down, tears glinting. "You right. And if I could take that back, I would. I just didn't want you to carry more of my mess."

Layla leaned forward. "That's not your choice to make. Love don't work like that. If we're doing this, we carry it together — all of it."

He met her eyes, the shame softening into gratitude. "So... you still want this?"

Layla hesitated. "I want *us*. But we starting over. No secrets, no shadows. Just truth."

He nodded slowly. "Then that's what you'll get."

The guard called "Time!" — but this time, when she stood, she reached across the table, touching his hand.

Her touch was shaky, but real.

"Don't make me regret forgiving you," she whispered.

"I won't," he said. "Not ever again."

The Letter That Followed

That night, Layla wrote one more letter. This time, it wasn't angry or broken — it was honest.

> *Marcus,*
>
> *The truth didn't break us — it just stripped away what wasn't solid. Now we get to build something that can't be shaken.*

Next time you're scared to tell me something, remember this: I can handle your truth, but I can't heal from your silence.

When Marcus read it days later, he pressed it against his heart, whispering, "God, thank You for this woman."

He finally understood: love wasn't about being perfect.

It was about being real enough to rebuild when the truth finally showed up.

Chapter 15 – Forgiveness in Chains

Forgiveness doesn't come like lightning.

It comes slow — quiet — like dawn through a window that hasn't been opened in years.

That's how it came to Marcus.

Not through a sermon, or a letter, but in the stillness of one morning when he woke up before the lights flicked on. He sat on his bunk, staring at his hands — rough, scarred, still shaking sometimes from the weight of everything they'd done.

He whispered into the silence, "I forgive myself."

Then he said it again, louder. "I forgive myself."

And for the first time, he actually meant it.

A Change in His Spirit

That week, people started noticing the difference.

Rico told him, "Man, you smiling more. What, you win the lottery or something?"

Marcus laughed. "Nah. I just stopped losin' sleep over what I can't change."

He began spending more time in the chapel, not because he was trying to prove anything, but because peace had become his favorite kind of freedom.

He helped the chaplain organize evening talks about growth and redemption. He listened when the younger guys vented, even when they reminded him of his old self — reckless, angry, half-alive.

"Y'all think being hard make you real," he told them one night. "But being real mean facing what's ugly and choosing not to stay there."

The room went quiet. Nobody argued.

That night, Marcus wrote Layla a letter:

> *Baby,*
>
> *I used to think forgiveness was about being let off the hook. But it's really about letting go of the chains you put on yourself. Every time I tell the truth, I feel lighter. Every time you choose to stay, I feel loved different — like maybe God ain't done with me after all.*

Layla's Healing Begins

Layla read his letter sitting outside on her porch, wrapped in her robe, coffee steaming beside her.

His words didn't erase the pain — but they softened it.

She'd spent nights replaying his confession, wondering if staying made her weak.

But now she realized — forgiveness wasn't weakness; it was strength in disguise.

That weekend, she went to see his mother.

Mrs. Henderson's health had stabilized. When Layla walked in, the older woman smiled, her eyes knowing.

"You forgave him," she said simply.

Layla nodded. "I'm learning how."

"That's enough. Forgiving don't mean forgetting. It mean remembering without the hurt controlling you."

Those words stayed with her. That night, she wrote Marcus back:

You were right — forgiveness set me free too. I don't have to pretend everything's okay. I just have to keep showing up until my heart catches up to my faith.

New Rhythms, Same Love

Their letters changed again after that.

Less pain. More purpose.

They wrote about plans — his reentry programs, her dream of opening a wellness clinic for women who'd been through loss and struggle.

When they spoke on the phone, there was laughter again — real, deep laughter that came from peace, not pretending.

One night, he said, "You ever think maybe this was all part of the plan?"

Layla smiled. "You mean God using prison as a love story?"

He chuckled. "Something like that. Maybe He just needed me still long enough to learn how to love you right."

Her heart swelled. "Then don't waste the lesson."

"I won't."

And somehow, for both of them, that promise felt like a new kind of freedom.

The next few months passed differently.

Time no longer dragged; it moved with purpose.

Marcus wasn't just serving his sentence — he was serving *others.*

He started mentoring a group of younger inmates officially through the facility's reentry program. The chaplain called it "Men of Renewal."

Every Thursday evening, they gathered in the chapel, a circle of folding chairs and quiet hearts trying to unlearn survival.

Marcus opened each session with the same words:

"We can't rewrite where we been, but we can decide where we go next."

Some nights the men argued. Some nights they cried. But every night, they showed up.

And that was progress.

Letters That Taught and Healed

Layla became part of the group from a distance. Marcus read her letters to the men, her words about patience, faith, and rebuilding.

> *"Every person who's broken still has purpose,"* she wrote in one.

> *"Sometimes you just need someone who believes you can start again."*

The men listened, some nodding, some silent — but her words always hit home.

After one session, Rico said, "Yo, she sound like a preacher."

Marcus smiled. "She's more than that — she's the reason I believe I can do better."

Later, he wrote her:

You don't even know how many brothers you touch in here. Your words reach farther than these walls. You out there building me, and I'm in here building them. It's like God using both of us at the same time.

When Layla read that letter, her hands trembled — not from sadness, but from awe. She realized love could ripple farther than she ever imagined.

Layla's Mirror Moment

One morning, as Layla was getting ready for work, she caught her reflection in the mirror — tired eyes, soft lines, but stronger than she'd ever looked.

She thought about all the times she'd blamed herself for staying, for loving, for hoping. People had whispered behind her back, called her naive, said she was wasting her best years.

But she finally understood — she hadn't been stuck. She'd been *becoming*.

That night, she sat on her bed, journal open, and wrote a letter she never planned to send.

Dear Me,

You did your best. You loved even when it hurt. You didn't quit when it got hard. Stop punishing yourself for being human. You don't need to be perfect to be worthy.

She read it aloud, then folded it neatly and tucked it between the pages of her Bible.

A prayer, a promise, and a release — all in one.

Marcus's Test of Faith

Inside, Marcus's leadership didn't go unnoticed.

The warden himself stopped him one afternoon. "Heard you been turning that chapel into something good."

Marcus nodded humbly. "Just trying to make use of the time, sir."

"Well," the warden said, "keep it up. Word like that travels."

That night, Marcus wrote Layla again:

They say freedom starts in your mind. If that's true, I think I been free for a while now. I just gotta walk it out when I get home.

Layla read that line over and over.

Free for a while now.

She smiled, whispering, "That's what forgiveness really is."

The Day of Stillness

Sunday morning, Layla lit a candle in her living room, gospel humming low in the background. She closed her eyes and whispered, "Thank You."

Not for the pain. But for what it had taught her — strength, endurance, patience, and love that didn't depend on circumstance.

Across miles, Marcus was sitting in the chapel at that exact moment, head bowed, whispering the same prayer.

"Thank You."

Neither of them knew it, but their hearts had finally met in the same peace.

Forgiveness — not as an act, but as a home they both could live in.

Chapter 16 – Counting Down the Days

The letter came on a Tuesday morning.

Layla had just poured her coffee when she noticed the thick brown envelope on the doormat, the one stamped *Tennessee Department of Corrections.*

Her stomach dropped. For a split second, she feared bad news.

But when she tore it open and read the first line, her knees nearly gave out.

> *"Inmate Marcus Henderson has been approved for early release. Expected date: March 14."*

She clutched the paper to her chest, whispering, "Oh my God."

Her hands trembled as tears of pure relief filled her eyes. After years of praying, hoping, and holding on, freedom finally had a date.

She sat down, breath shaking, and whispered, "We made it."

The Call That Changed Everything

When the phone rang later that day, she didn't even say hello.

"They gave it to you, didn't they?" she blurted out.

Marcus laughed — that deep, quiet laugh she'd missed so much. "You already know."

Layla covered her mouth, half crying, half laughing. "March 14? That's two months!"

"Sixty-three days," he said. "I been counting since they told me."

She could hear the emotion in his voice — not just joy, but disbelief.

He'd waited years for this moment, and now it was real.

"Marcus," she whispered, "you're coming home."

He paused. "Yeah… I'm comin' home."

For a long time, neither spoke. The silence was full — heavy with all the memories that had carried them here: the visits, the letters, the tears, the prayers.

Finally, Marcus said softly, "You still want me, Lay? After all this?"

Her answer came without hesitation. "More than ever."

The World Keeps Moving

The weeks that followed felt like a dream.

Layla threw herself into preparation — cleaning, organizing, making space for the life they'd been building on paper.

She scrubbed floors, repainted the kitchen, and even started shopping for small things — towels, new sheets, fresh curtains. It wasn't about appearances; it was about creating a place that felt like peace.

Maya teased her constantly. "You acting like you about to get married."

Layla smiled. "Maya, you don't get it. When you wait for something this long, even a clean pillowcase feels like a blessing."

Still, there were moments of fear.

Late at night, she'd catch herself wondering: *What if he's changed too much?*

What if we don't fit anymore?

Then she'd remember his voice over the phone, steady and warm:

"I ain't the same man, but I still love the same woman."

And that was enough to calm her doubts.

Marcus's Countdown

Inside, Marcus's life had turned into a calendar.

Each morning, he marked off another square with a small "." He counted by weeks, not days — it felt less painful that way.

He'd already sent most of his belonging's home in boxes — books, letters, and the Bible Layla had mailed him three years ago, still full of her handwritten notes.

Every night before lights out, he'd sit on the edge of his bunk, holding one of her old letters, whispering, "Almost home."

Rico slapped him on the shoulder one evening. "You ready, old man?"

Marcus grinned. "Been ready."

Rico laughed. "Don't forget about us little people when you get out."

Marcus chuckled. "You ain't little, bro. You next."

The two bumped fists. It wasn't just brotherhood — it was faith in motion.

Dreams of Freedom

Sometimes Marcus would close his eyes and imagine it:

The feel of real air that wasn't rationed by walls. The sound of Layla's laugh without a phone delay. The warmth of her hand in his, no guard watching.

He'd picture her waiting outside those gates in something bright — yellow, maybe, the color she wore that first day at the cookout. The thought alone was enough to make him smile in his sleep.

In one of his last letters to her, he wrote:

> *You ever love somebody so deep that time itself start working for you instead of against you? That's what this feels like. Every second got your name in it.*

> When Layla read that, she pressed the paper to her lips and whispered, "Come home safe."

The final week came faster than either of them expected.

For years, time had moved like molasses. Now it sprinted, each sunrise a drumbeat in their chests.

Marcus could feel it in the air — that strange mix of excitement and fear that comes right before freedom. His world had been the same four walls for so long, he wasn't sure how to breathe outside of them.

The Last Night Inside

The night before his release, the prison felt different.

Quieter. Almost respectful. Like even the walls knew he was leaving.

Marcus lay awake staring at the ceiling; hands folded behind his head. Every noise sounded sharper — the rattle of the air vent, the shuffle of guards, the faint snores from nearby bunks. He had memorized these sounds for years, and now he was about to leave them behind.

He thought about everything he'd learned.

About who he used to be.

About who he'd become.

And about the woman who'd carried him through every bit of the in-between.

Rico's voice broke the silence. "You gon' sleep or just stare at the ceiling all night?"

Marcus chuckled. "You act like I ain't been waitin' for this day since forever."

"Still wild though," Rico said, turning over. "You really made it out clean."

Marcus smiled faintly. "By grace, bro. Only by grace."

When lights-out hit, Marcus whispered one last prayer.

"God, don't let me waste this second chance. I'm ready to live right."

Layla's Night of Restlessness

That same night, miles away, Layla couldn't sleep either.

She'd cleaned the apartment three times. The bed was made, the fridge was stocked, candles were lined up on the counter — everything ready, but her nerves still hummed.

Maya peeked into her room. "You still up?"

Layla laughed softly. "Couldn't sleep if I tried."

"You nervous?"

Layla nodded. "Excited. Scared. Happy. All of it."

Maya sat beside her, handing her a folded note. "I wrote this for him. Tell him I'm proud too."

Layla's eyes filled with tears. "You growing up, girl."

Maya grinned. "Guess I had a good example."

They hugged tight, both of them knowing that tomorrow, life would finally shift — again.

Dawn of the Day

The sky was barely pink when Marcus stood in front of the mirror, dressed in the clothes Layla had mailed him weeks ago — a clean white tee, dark jeans, and sneakers that still looked foreign on his feet

He ran his hands over his head, exhaled deeply, and whispered, "Let's go."

At 6:43 a.m., the heavy doors opened with a slow groan.

Marcus stepped out, blinking against the sunrise — a free man.

He could smell the air, thick with spring and possibility.

And then, he saw her.

Layla stood by the car, sunlight spilling across her yellow sundress — the same color as the day they met.

Her eyes were already wet, her hands trembling as she took a step forward.

Marcus dropped his duffel bag and closed the space between them in seconds.

When she fell into his arms, the world finally stopped moving.

For a long time, neither spoke. Just the sound of their breathing, and the weight of years melting away.

Finally, Marcus whispered, "You smell like home."

Layla laughed through tears. "You feel like peace."

The Drive Home

They rode with the windows down, music low — old-school R&B humming through the speakers.

For a while, they didn't talk. They didn't need to. Just being together felt loud enough.

At one red light, Marcus reached over and took her hand.

"I ain't never gon' stop thanking you," he said quietly.

"You don't have to," she replied. "Just live the life we prayed for."

He smiled, thumb brushing her knuckles. "That's the plan."

As the city skyline faded behind them, Marcus rolled the window down farther, letting the wind hit his face.

"Man," he said, laughing, "I forgot what real air feels like."

Layla grinned. "Get used to it. That's freedom."

And as the sun climbed higher, painting gold across the road ahead, both of them finally exhaled — together.

Chapter 17 – The Homecoming

Freedom didn't feel like fireworks.

It felt like stillness — like standing in sunlight after years underground.

For Marcus, every sound, every smell, every color hit harder than he remembered. The rustle of trees, the hum of traffic, even the taste of real coffee from the gas station on the way home — all of it felt like a miracle.

He sat in the passenger seat watching the world blur past, whispering under his breath, "I'm really out."

Layla smiled without looking away from the road. "You're really out."

He turned toward her. "You sure this ain't a dream?"

She laughed softly. "If it is, don't wake me up."

Back at the Apartment

When they pulled into the parking lot, Marcus froze for a moment. He'd imagined this scene a thousand times — walking up the steps, turning the knob, stepping into something that wasn't temporary.

Layla opened the door for him and said quietly, "Welcome home."

The apartment smelled like vanilla and fresh paint. New curtains hung by the window, the couch was rearranged, and on the kitchen counter sat a basket full of snacks and toiletries with a note that read, *"Fresh start."*

Marcus's eyes softened. "You did all this?"

She shrugged. "Just wanted you to walk into peace."

He smiled, that slow grin that used to undo her completely. "You always did know how to build peace outta chaos."

He walked slowly through the small space — touched the wall, the counter, the table — like each thing was proof this was real.

When he reached the living room, he stopped in front of the photo of her and Maya. "She taller now," he said.

Layla laughed. "Taller and nosier."

"Good," he said. "Means she growing."

The First Real Meal

Layla cooked like she was feeding a king — baked chicken, mac and cheese, greens, cornbread.

Marcus sat at the table watching her, the way she moved, the rhythm of home in every gesture.

"You sure you remember how to eat real food?" she teased.

He grinned. "I might need a refresher."

They ate in comfortable silence for a while, only breaking it for small talk and laughter. Marcus kept glancing around, soaking everything in — the light through the window, the sound of her humming.

Halfway through the meal, he set his fork down.

"I forgot how good simple feels."

Layla smiled softly. "That's what we prayed for. Simple, not perfect."

He reached across the table, his fingers brushing hers. "You really waited for me."

"I told you I would."

He nodded. "I know. But seein' it — that's different."

Seeing Family Again

Later that evening, they drove across town to his mother's house.

Mrs. Henderson opened the door before they even knocked, her voice trembling, "My baby."

Marcus stepped forward, eyes wet, and she wrapped him in her arms. Neither spoke — just held on, years of distance collapsing between them.

Layla stood back, tears streaming as she watched.

When they finally sat down, Mrs. Henderson cupped his face in her hands. "You look like peace, son."

Marcus laughed through his tears. "Trying to be."

"You doing better than that," she said. "You *being* better."

She turned to Layla, smiling. "Thank you for not letting go when it got heavy."

Layla squeezed her hand. "He gave me just enough reason to hold on."

The three of them sat there for hours — eating, reminiscing, praying. The air was thick with gratitude and grace.

Before they left, his mother handed him the old photo Layla had kept — the one of him as a boy with the gap-toothed grin.

"Don't forget who you were before the world tried to change you," she said.

Marcus nodded, tucking it carefully into his pocket. "I won't."

Late-Night Stillness

That night, back at Layla's apartment, they sat on the porch.

The moon hung low and gold, the air soft with the hum of summer.

Neither said much. Words weren't needed — not tonight.

Marcus leaned back, eyes on the stars. "You ever notice how the sky look bigger when you free?"

Layla smiled faintly. "Maybe it's always been that big. You just get to see it now."

He reached over, took her hand, and whispered, "I ain't never letting go."

She turned to him, her voice quiet but steady. "Then don't."

And for the first time in years, they both felt whole — not because everything was fixed, but because everything that mattered was finally *real*.

The first few days after Marcus came home felt almost sacred.

Every sunrise looked different. Every sound felt alive.

He'd wake before dawn, sit by the window, and just breathe — no guards, no roll call, no cell door slamming shut. Just air and quiet.

Layla would find him there sometimes, lost in thought, hands clasped together.

"You okay?" she'd whisper.

He'd smile faintly. "Just makin' sure this is still real."

Learning the New World

Freedom, Marcus learned quickly, was beautiful but strange.

The world had changed while he was gone.

Touch screens replaced buttons, cash was rare, and everybody seemed to talk to their phones more than to each other.

On his first solo errand, he walked into a corner store, froze in front of the self-checkout machine, and muttered, "Man, what is this?"

The teenage cashier laughed kindly. "You good, bro. Just scan it here."

Marcus nodded, fumbling with the scanner until the beep sounded.

He grinned. "Aight, progress."

When he got back, Layla was waiting by the window.

"How'd it go?"

He shrugged. "Didn't rob the store, didn't break the machine. So I'd say good."

She laughed, pulling him close. "You'll get it. Just take your time."

But not everything came easy. Sometimes the noise of the city made him flinch. Sirens pulled old memories to the surface. Crowds felt too close. And at night, when the house got quiet, he'd wake up thinking someone was calling his name for count.

Layla learned to soothe him without smothering. She'd touch his arm gently and whisper, "You're home, baby. Nobody's coming for you."

And slowly, the panic would fade.

The Job Hunt

Finding work was another mountain.

He filled out application after application, each one asking the same question: *Have you ever been convicted of a felony?*

He hated that box. It felt like a wall built just for him.

One afternoon, after another rejection email, he tossed his phone down.

"They don't even look past the first line," he said. "Soon as they see that word, it's over."

Layla sat beside him. "Then we'll find someone who looks at you, not your past."

"That's easier said than done."

"Yeah," she said softly. "But we've done harder."

Her faith in him didn't fix everything, but it gave him the strength to keep trying.

A week later, an old friend from church connected him to a mechanic who needed help detailing cars. It wasn't much money, but it was honest work — and it smelled like freedom.

The first day back in a garage, Marcus wiped his hands on a rag, looked around at the grease, the hum of engines, and thought, *This is where rebuilding starts.*

Old Temptations

Not everyone was happy to see him doing good.

A few old faces from the block started calling, testing him with the same easy money that had wrecked his life before.

One night, his phone lit up with a number he knew too well.

He stared at it until the ringing stopped.

Layla, washing dishes, noticed his tense shoulders.

"Who was that?"

He hesitated. "Nobody that belongs in this new chapter."

She dried her hands, walked over, and kissed his cheek. "That's right. Let the old chapter stay closed."

He nodded, deleting the number without another thought.

Later, lying beside her, he whispered, "I ain't never risking this again."

She smiled in the dark. "Then you're already winning."

Family Adjustments

Maya adored Marcus but had questions — too many sometimes.

"Did you have a bed like this in there?"

"Could you watch TV?"

"Did you fight people?"

Marcus laughed. "You watch too much Netflix."

"I'm just sayin'," she teased. "You seem way too calm for somebody who been through all that."

He grinned. "Calm ain't weakness. It's peace."

Over time, Maya began to see him not as the man who went away, but as part of their everyday rhythm — the one who cooked breakfast on Sundays, fixed the squeaky cabinet, and told her to keep her grades up.

Relearning Intimacy

For Layla and Marcus, even closeness had to be relearned.

In prison, touch was a luxury. Now, it was everywhere — a hand on her back as she passed, a kiss on her shoulder while she cooked.

Some nights, they lay awake just talking — no glass between them, no time limits, no guards.

Marcus would trace his fingers along her arm and whisper, "You don't know how many nights I dreamed about this."

She'd smile against his chest. "Then dream with your eyes open now."

It wasn't always smooth. Sometimes he'd pull away without meaning to — used to solitude, to silence.

Layla didn't push; she simply reminded him, "You don't have to unlearn love. You just gotta remember it."

And slowly, they both began to remember.

Freedom in Motion

One Saturday, months after his release, Marcus stood outside the garage, wiping sweat from his forehead. His boss handed him a set of keys.

"You've been solid, man. How you feel about running your own crew?"

Marcus froze. "You serious?"

"As a heart attack. You earned it."

When he got home and told Layla, she jumped into his arms, laughing through tears.

"I told you God wasn't done with you," she said.

He smiled. "Guess He just needed me to trust Him first."

That night, they drove out to the park where they'd had their first picnic years ago. The same oak tree stood tall, the same sunset burned orange across the water.

Marcus looked over at her and whispered, "You ever think about how far we came?"

Layla nodded. "Every day."

He took her hand. "Then let's keep going. Together."

Chapter 18 – Adjusting to Freedom

Freedom sounded beautiful but living it took work.

Marcus quickly learned that getting out was just the beginning. The real challenge was staying out — staying focused, staying grounded, and staying faithful to the peace he'd promised Layla.

For Layla, it was about balance. She wanted to protect him, but she also knew he needed space to breathe — to feel like a man again, not a project.

They were learning each other all over again. Love after prison was different. It was louder, softer, more complicated, and more fragile all at once.

The Weight of Routine

Every Monday morning, Marcus met with his parole officer, a woman named Ms. Jennings.

She was tough, no-nonsense, but fair.

"Stay clean, stay on time, and stay working," she told him. "You do that, and we won't have no problems."

He nodded each time. "Yes, ma'am."

Still, every meeting made him nervous. Even walking into the office brought back that old tightness in his chest. The sound of keys, the smell of disinfectant — it all echoed the years he spent locked away.

Layla noticed it.

"You always tense after those meetings," she said one day.

He rubbed the back of his neck. "It's like my body don't know the difference between check-in and lockdown yet."

She reached across the table, squeezing his hand. "One day, it will."

He smiled softly. "Yeah. One day."

New Struggles, Old Triggers

Money was tight.

The job at the garage was steady, but not enough for all the bills. Layla had picked up extra shifts at the clinic, coming home bone-tired but still smiling.

One night, Marcus found her asleep at the table, paperwork spread around her.

He gently lifted her head and said, "Baby, you can't work yourself into the ground."

She stirred, half-asleep. "I'm just... trying to keep us ahead."

He whispered, "We already winning. Look at us — we here."

She smiled weakly. "You always know how to say the right thing."

"Not always," he said, kissing her forehead. "But I mean it."

Still, deep down, Marcus felt a weight he couldn't shake. He wanted to do more — provide more, be more. Every man he knew measured himself by what he could bring home, and right now, he felt like he was coming up short.

That pressure simmered quietly until it started showing in his mood.

Layla noticed the long silences, the restless pacing, the faraway look in his eyes.

"Talk to me," she said one night. "Don't shut down on me now."

He sighed. "I'm just trying to figure out how to be normal again."

She frowned. "Normal's overrated. Just be real."

Her words hit deeper than she knew.

The Past at the Door

One afternoon, while Layla was at work, someone knocked on their door.

Marcus opened it and froze.

Standing there was Dre — an old associate from his past. Dressed in gold chains, designer sneakers, and the same street charm Marcus used to wear like armor.

"Damn, bro," Dre said, grinning. "They really let you out."

Marcus nodded slowly. "Yeah. Been out a few months."

"Good for you. You lookin' solid. You still on your grind?"

"Yeah," Marcus said cautiously. "Workin' at a shop now."

Dre chuckled. "Man, you too smart to be detailing cars. I got moves lined up — quick money, no risk."

Marcus shook his head. "Ain't no such thing as no risk. I learned that the hard way."

Dre's grin faded. "You really lettin' the system tame you?"

Marcus's tone hardened. "I'm lettin' peace keep me alive."

Before Dre could answer, Marcus closed the door. He leaned against it, breathing heavy. The sound of that door clicking shut felt like redemption — and temptation at the same time.

When Layla came home later, she found him quiet, deep in thought.

"What's wrong?" she asked.

He hesitated, then told her everything.

She exhaled slowly. "I'm proud of you."

"For what?"

"For choosing peace over pride."

He smiled faintly. "It ain't easy."

She touched his chest. "It's not supposed to be. Growth never is."

The Mirror Moment

That night, Marcus stood in front of the bathroom mirror long after Layla had fallen asleep.

He studied his reflection — the same eyes, same scars, but a different man staring back.

He thought about the old Marcus — the one who chased fast money, the one who thought love couldn't last behind bars.

Then he thought about Layla — how she'd waited, prayed, and believed even when he didn't.

"Don't mess this up," he whispered to himself.

"Not again."

He turned off the light, climbed into bed beside her, and wrapped his arm around her waist.

In her sleep, she reached for his hand like she'd been doing it forever.

And just like that, the noise in his head finally quieted.

The calm didn't last forever.

Freedom came with new tests — not the kind that came from guards or concrete walls, but from life itself.

The closer Marcus got to stability, the more life seemed to challenge it.

Bills, expectations, exhaustion — they all pressed in from every side.

And in the middle of it, Layla and Marcus had to remember that love wasn't just about surviving together. It was about *living* together.

Growing Pains

Layla started to notice small cracks in their rhythm.

Marcus had good days — easy smiles, steady laughter, that old spark in his eyes — but he also had days where silence hung over him like a shadow.

He'd sit on the porch for hours, staring at nothing, his mind somewhere she couldn't follow.

One evening, she stepped outside, wiping her hands on a towel.

"You okay?"

He nodded without looking up. "Yeah."

"Marcus…"

He exhaled, finally meeting her gaze. "It's just—sometimes I feel like I don't belong nowhere. Not in that world, not out here. Like I left one box just to live in another."

Layla sat beside him. "You belong right here. With me."

He smiled faintly. "You always know what to say."

"Because I know you," she said softly. "And I'm not gonna let you drift away just because the world moves different now."

He took her hand, eyes full of quiet gratitude. "You saved me, you know that?"

She shook her head. "Nah. You saved yourself. I just reminded you, you're worth it."

The Argument

But love — even real love — isn't perfect.

It happened on a Thursday.

Layla came home from work exhausted, her scrubs wrinkled, her patience thin. The sink was full of dishes, and Marcus was sitting on the couch scrolling through job listings on his phone.

"I thought you said you were gonna take care of the kitchen," she said.

He looked up. "I will."

"You said that yesterday too."

"Lay, I been filling out applications all afternoon."

"And the dishes been sitting there all afternoon too."

The tension snapped fast.

"I'm doing the best I can," he said, standing up.

"I know you are," she said, voice trembling, "but sometimes it feels like I'm carrying everything — the bills, the house, your stress, mine—"

"You think I don't feel that? You think I don't wake up every day wanting to do more?"

Silence. Heavy. Cutting.

Layla's eyes filled with tears. "That's not what I meant."

Marcus rubbed his temples, pacing. "I know. I just… I get tired of feeling like I'm still proving myself."

She walked over slowly, placing her hand on his chest. "You don't have to prove anything to me, Marcus. You already did that when you came home."

He looked at her, eyes softening. "I just don't want to fail you."

"Then don't shut me out," she whispered. "That's the only way we lose."

He pulled her into his arms, holding her tight.

"I'm sorry," he murmured against her hair.

"I know," she said. "Me too."

They stood there in the middle of the living room — tired, flawed, and in love — proving that sometimes, holding it down meant simply not walking away.

Faith in Motion

Sunday morning found them sitting side by side in church, fingers intertwined.

It had been a while since Marcus had stepped into a sanctuary. The choir's voices filled the air, and he felt something stir deep inside him — a calm he hadn't felt since before the streets, before the time.

When the pastor said, *"God doesn't waste your pain — He repurposes it,"* Marcus closed his eyes.

After service, Layla looked up at him. "You okay?"

He smiled. "Yeah. Just realizing I ain't where I used to be."

She nodded. "That's growth."

He turned toward her, eyes bright with something new — hope. "I think I'm ready to start something for real, Lay. A business. A shop. Something with my name on it."

Her face lit up. "You serious?"

"Dead serious. I been saving a little. And I know a couple of people who'll help me get started."

"Then let's do it," she said without hesitation.

"You mean it?"

"Marcus, I've believed in you when all you had was a dream and a jumpsuit. Why would I stop now?"

He laughed softly, emotion thick in his throat. "You the realest woman I ever met."

"And don't you forget it," she teased, brushing his cheek.

Still Learning Each Other

Weeks turned into months.

The rhythm between them settled again — not perfect, but peaceful.

Marcus would come home from the shop smelling like oil and sweat, and Layla would still be in her scrubs, hair tied up, humming while she cooked.

They'd talk about their days, laugh about little things, and sometimes just sit in silence, letting the quiet feel like comfort instead of distance.

One night, as they sat on the couch, Marcus looked over at her and said, "You ever think about how love is just… work that don't feel like work when it's right?"

Layla smiled. "Yeah. It's choosing each other every day — even when it's hard."

He nodded. "Then I choose you. Every day."

She leaned in, her forehead resting against his. "Good. Because I'm not done holding you down yet."

And for the first time since freedom began, Marcus believed that maybe, just maybe, they could make it all the way.

Chapter 19 – The Test of Trust

Peace had a rhythm now.

Marcus woke early, left for the garage, came home smelling like sweat, grease, and purpose. Layla's shifts at the clinic were long, but she no longer dreaded them. They were both building, climbing — side by side.

But success has a way of attracting attention.

And sometimes, not all attention comes with good intentions.

The Spotlight

Marcus's reputation spread fast. Word around the city was that *the ex-con who turned his life around* was running one of the cleanest, most honest detailing crews in town.

Customers liked his work, but what really pulled people in was his story.

Soon, local reporters wanted to interview him for a feature about second chances. The article ran with a photo of him standing in front of a car, sleeves rolled up, a proud smile on his face.

Layla showed it to Maya at the kitchen table. "Look at your brother!" she said proudly.

Maya grinned. "Okay, Mr. Community Hero!"

But as proud as she was, Layla couldn't ignore the sudden shift — the way women at church whispered when Marcus walked in, or how new female customers lingered too long at the garage.

Marcus brushed it off. "People just curious, Lay. That's all."

"Yeah," she said quietly. "Curious is one thing. Flirting is another."

He laughed, pulling her close. "You know where my heart stay."

She smiled — but deep down, a seed of unease had already been planted.

Rumors Begin

It started small.

A woman named Tasha — a client who'd been coming to the garage more than most — began leaving comments under Marcus's social posts. Compliments turned into emojis, emojis turned into heart eyes.

Marcus ignored them at first.

But one afternoon, she stopped by with lunch for the crew. When Marcus tried to turn it down, she winked. "You gotta eat, right?"

His coworkers laughed, teasing. "Boy, you got fans now!"

Marcus shook his head. "Ain't nobody got time for that."

Still, someone snapped a photo of her handing him the bag — and by that evening, the picture made its way to Layla's phone with the message:

"You sure your man's keeping it clean?"

Her chest tightened. She didn't want to believe it. She didn't even *really* think it was anything. But the image hit hard — not because she thought he'd done something wrong, but because she'd seen this kind of story before.

That night, she barely spoke at dinner.

Marcus noticed. "You good?"

She nodded. "Just tired."

He didn't press — not yet.

The Breaking Point

Two nights later, Layla's phone buzzed again — another message, this time a screenshot of Tasha commenting, *"My favorite detailer 😊"*

Layla sat in bed, staring at it, heart pounding.

When Marcus came in from the shower, towel around his neck, she turned the phone toward him. "You wanna explain this?"

He froze. "Explain what?"

"This woman posting hearts under your pictures, bringing you lunch like y'all got something going on."

He sighed. "Layla, it's not what you think."

"Then what is it?"

"She a client — nothing more. I can't control what people post."

She stood up. "You can control what kind of boundaries you set."

He ran a hand over his head, trying to stay calm. "You really think I'd throw away everything we built? After all this?"

"I don't *want* to think that," she said, voice shaking. "But I also don't want to look stupid."

That word cut deep. *Stupid.*

Marcus took a step back. "So now you think I'm out here playin' you?"

"I think I've seen too many good men fall back into bad habits when life got comfortable."

He stared at her for a long moment — anger, hurt, and disappointment flickering all at once.

"I been fighting to prove I ain't that man no more," he said quietly. "But I can't prove it if you already made up your mind."

Then he walked out onto the porch, the screen door slamming behind him.

Reflection in the Dark

Layla sat on the edge of the bed, hands trembling.

She hated that they'd come this far just to hit another wall. She knew Marcus wasn't the man he used to be, but old fear had a way of creeping in when love started to feel too good.

Out on the porch, Marcus lit a cigarette he didn't even want. The smoke curled up into the night sky as he whispered to himself, "Why's it always gotta be a test?"

He thought about all the people waiting to see him fail, the ones who said men like him didn't change.

He thought about Layla — how much she'd sacrificed for him, and how much it would hurt if she stopped believing now.

After a long silence, he crushed the cigarette under his shoe, went back inside, and sat on the edge of the bed beside her.

"I don't want no space between us," he said quietly.

She looked up, tears spilling over. "Then help me trust you."

He nodded. "I will. Every day if I have to."

And for the first time that night, the air between them began to soften.

The morning after their argument, the air between them felt heavy — not angry, just quiet.

Layla moved around the kitchen in silence, fixing her coffee. Marcus sat at the table, scrolling through his phone, his jaw tight.

When she set his mug down beside him, he said softly, "I deleted her number."

Layla froze. "You didn't have to—"

"Yes, I did," he interrupted gently. "Because peace don't come with mixed signals. And I want peace — with you."

She looked at him, eyes softening. "Marcus…"

He reached across the table, covering her hand with his. "I know I can't control how people see me. But I *can* control how I move. I can't let nobody question what we built, least of all you."

Tears welled in her eyes. "I just—sometimes it's hard. I waited for you through everything. And I guess part of me still gets scared of losing you now that the world's finally seeing what I saw all along."

Marcus's voice was quiet, full of love. "You ain't never gotta compete with the world, Lay. You *are* my world."

The words broke something inside her — not pain, but relief.

She took a deep breath, nodded, and whispered, "Okay. Let's start fresh."

He smiled faintly. "Deal."

Proving with Actions

Marcus didn't just talk — he moved different.

He stopped posting on social media altogether, focusing instead on growing his business and rebuilding his credibility one day at a time.

He set up boundaries at the shop too. No personal conversations with clients. No "friendly" favors. If someone crossed the line, he redirected them politely but firmly.

"Appreciate the business," he'd say with a smile, "but I keep it strictly professional."

Word got around, and soon, the teasing from coworkers stopped. Marcus carried himself like a man who knew exactly what he stood for.

Layla noticed.

When she dropped by one afternoon with lunch, she watched him work — sleeves rolled, jaw set, focus unshakable.

She could tell he wasn't just trying to *look* faithful. He was *being faithful*.

When their eyes met across the shop, he smiled — not flirtatious, not performative. Just real.

And for the first time in weeks, Layla's heart finally unclenched.

Layla's Own Reflection

Later that night, Layla stood in front of the bathroom mirror brushing her hair, studying her reflection.

She realized she'd spent so long being strong that she'd forgotten how to *feel safe*.

Marcus wasn't perfect, but he was trying. And that meant she had to try too — to trust again without letting her fears write the story.

She thought about all the nights she'd prayed for this man, all the tears she'd cried waiting for him to come home.

Now that he was here, maybe the real test wasn't him. Maybe it was her — learning to stop living in survival mode.

She set the brush down, looked at herself, and whispered, "You're allowed to relax now. You're safe."

Small Gestures, Big Healing

Over the next few weeks, the tension began to fade.

They found their rhythm again — dinners, laughter, small moments that reminded them why they'd fought so hard to get here.

Marcus started leaving her little notes around the apartment — handwritten on scrap paper, tucked into her purse, her lunch bag, even her Bible.

"For every day I made you cry, I'll spend a lifetime making you smile."

"You're my peace, not my problem."

"Thank you for still choosing me."

Layla kept every one.

In return, she started showing up at his shop once a week with lunch and that same yellow sundress — his favorite. She'd kiss his cheek in front of the crew, just to remind the world where his heart lived.

The men teased him relentlessly, but Marcus didn't care.

"She held me down when I had nothin'," he told them once. "So, she gets to walk in here like the queen she is."

The Big Decision

One evening, while they sat on the porch watching the sun dip low, Marcus turned to her, nervous.

"So, I been thinking…"

Layla smiled. "That sounds dangerous."

He chuckled. "Nah, this one's good. I wanna open my own place. Not just a shop — a business with my name on it. Something that stands for second chances."

Her eyes widened. "You serious?"

"As a heart attack. I been saving. Got a line on a small space downtown. I wanna call it *Second Chance Repairs.*"

Layla's eyes filled with tears — proud ones. "That's perfect."

"You think I can pull it off?"

She leaned in, cupping his face. "Marcus, you've already done the hardest part — you changed your life. The rest is just following through."

He smiled, voice thick with emotion. "Then I guess we really made it, huh?"

She nodded. "Almost. But the best part's still coming."

He raised an eyebrow. "What's that?"

Layla grinned. "The life we're about to live after all this work."

The Quiet Victory

That night, after dinner, Marcus stood outside looking up at the stars — the same way he used to back in his cell.

Only now, the air was warm, the sky wide, and the woman he loved was asleep just inside their home.

He whispered, "Thank you," — not to anyone specific, but to everything that had carried him here.

To Layla. To grace. To patience. To time.

For the first time in his life, he wasn't fighting to prove he'd changed.

He was living like he already had.

Chapter 20 – A Love Worth Waiting For

The day *Second Chance Repairs* opened, the air buzzed with quiet excitement.

The shop wasn't big — three bays, a small office, and a hand-painted sign that Layla had helped design. But to Marcus, it was more than a business. It was proof that redemption didn't have to ask for permission.

He stood out front in a crisp black polo, wiping grease from his hands, staring at the sign with his name on it.

Marcus Henderson, Owner.

Layla came up behind him, slipping her arm around his waist.

"Looks good on you," she said softly.

He smiled. "Feels good too."

A few cars pulled in — regular customers, new faces, even some neighbors who'd just come to support. The mayor's assistant dropped off a small envelope with a note that read: *"Thank you for showing what second chances can look like."*

Marcus tucked it in his pocket, heart full.

The Grand Opening

Inside the shop, the smell of motor oil mixed with the sweetness of Layla's homemade cupcakes sitting on the counter. Music played low — old-school R&B, of course — and laughter bounced off the concrete walls.

Rico, now out and working with Marcus, raised a toast with a can of soda.

"To freedom, family, and the boss man finally doin' it right!"

Everyone clapped.

Marcus laughed, embarrassed but proud. "Ain't no boss without a team. We all in this together."

Layla smiled from the corner, watching him speak. His confidence wasn't loud — it was grounded. Humble. The kind that comes from surviving something and choosing not to waste it.

When he caught her eye, his voice softened. "And to the woman who taught me how to hold it down the right way."

The room went quiet, all eyes turning to Layla.

She laughed through her tears. "You always gotta make me cry in front of people."

Marcus grinned. "Wouldn't be us if I didn't."

The Simple Joys

Life settled into a rhythm again — but this time, it was steady, not survival.

Marcus spent his mornings at the shop, his afternoons doing paperwork, and his evenings home by Layla's side.

Sometimes, she'd bring Maya by after school to hang out. The three of them would eat dinner together, laughing until the food got cold.

Other nights, they'd sit on the porch, watching the world slow down. No noise. No drama. Just quiet peace.

One evening, Layla turned to him and said, "You ever think about how far we've come?"

He nodded. "Every time I wake up next to you."

She smiled, laying her head on his shoulder. "I used to pray God would send me a good man. I didn't know He was gonna make me wait for you through all that."

Marcus chuckled. "Guess He knew I needed fixing first."

They sat there in silence, the kind that didn't need words. Because some stories don't need retelling — just living.

Full-Circle Faith

Sunday mornings became sacred again. They'd sit in the same pew together, holding hands as the choir sang.

When the pastor asked Marcus to share his testimony one morning, he hesitated at first — then looked at Layla, who nodded.

He walked to the front, adjusting the mic. His voice was steady, full.

"I ain't got no fancy words. Just the truth. I lost a lot before I found myself. But the thing about grace is, it don't ask if you deserve it. It just meets you where you are."

He paused, glancing back at Layla. "And sometimes, grace looks like a woman who don't give up on you even when you gave up on yourself."

The church erupted in *amens.*

Layla wiped her tears, heart swelling with pride.

When he sat back down, she leaned over and whispered, "That was beautiful."

He smiled. "You the beautiful part."

A Proposal Rewritten by Time

That night, Marcus surprised her.

They drove to the same park where they'd had their first real date — the picnic under the oak tree, the place where he'd first told her about wanting a new life.

Now, the tree stood taller, its branches thicker, just like them.

Marcus took her hand and led her to the same spot. The grass was damp with evening dew, and fireflies blinked around them like tiny stars.

"What are we doing here?" she asked, smiling.

He reached into his pocket, pulling out a small black box.

Layla gasped softly. "Marcus…"

He opened it slowly — inside was a simple gold band, elegant and timeless.

"I ain't got no fancy speech," he said quietly. "You already heard all my words. But I want the rest of my life to be proof of them. You waited for me, prayed for me, carried me when I couldn't stand on my own. Now I want to spend forever giving that back to you."

Tears spilled freely down her cheeks. "Marcus, you don't even have to ask."

He smiled through his own tears. "Still gonna do it right, though."

He knelt down, the moonlight catching the ring. "Layla Carter — will you marry me?"

She laughed through sobs. "Yes. A thousand times yes."

He slid the ring on her finger, stood, and kissed her like the years had never passed — only grown stronger.

Under that same tree where it all began, they made a new promise: this time, not to hold it down through pain, but to build something that would never break again.

The morning of their wedding dawned soft and golden, sunlight spilling across the city like a blessing.

Layla stood before the mirror, her hands trembling slightly as Maya adjusted her veil.

"You nervous?" Maya asked, grinning.

Layla laughed, her voice thick with emotion. "More like grateful. Nervous left me years ago."

The dress wasn't extravagant — simple white lace, elegant but real. It fit her curves and her story. Every stitch felt like a prayer answered.

Maya wiped a tear before it could fall. "He's gonna lose it when he sees you."

Layla smiled, her eyes glassy. "Good. It's his turn to cry."

The Ceremony

The wedding took place at the same small church where Marcus had shared his testimony months before. The sanctuary was full — family, friends, and even a few of his old garage coworkers in their best shirts.

Gospel music filled the room as Marcus stood at the altar, his hands clasped tight, his heart thundering. Rico nudged him. "Breathe, bro. She coming."

And then she did.

When Layla stepped through the doors, time slowed. The world went quiet except for the soft rustle of her dress and the sound of Marcus's breath catching.

She looked radiant — not just beautiful, but *whole*.

Marcus's eyes glistened as she reached him. "You real?" he whispered, voice shaking.

Layla smiled softly. "Real as it gets."

The pastor's words flowed like poetry — about grace, redemption, and love that survives the impossible.

When Marcus slipped the ring onto her finger, he said, "This ain't just a ring. It's proof that waiting don't mean losing."

Layla's hands trembled as she placed his ring in return. "And loving don't mean hurting. It means healing, together."

When the pastor pronounced them husband and wife, the whole church erupted.

Marcus kissed her slow — deep — like he'd waited a lifetime for this one breath.

The Reception

The reception wasn't fancy. It didn't need to be.

Held at the same community center where Layla had once gone to grief counseling after her mother's death, it was decorated with string lights, wildflowers, and memories.

Marcus surprised her with a first dance song he'd chosen himself — *"Forever Mine" by* the O'Jays.

When the music started, he pulled her close and whispered, "Every lyric in this song? That's you."

Layla smiled through tears. "You always know how to make a moment."

"Gotta make up for lost time," he said, twirling her gently.

They danced slow, laughing, holding each other like the world had finally given them permission to exhale.

Maya gave a toast, her voice shaking: "To the two people who showed me that love ain't perfect, but it's real. And real love — it lasts."

Even Rico got choked up. "Man, I remember when this dude swore he'd never settle down. Look at him now — married and glowing!"

The crowd laughed, and Marcus wrapped an arm around Layla. "That glow's her fault," he said.

Building a Future

Weeks turned into months, and married life felt natural.

Layla still worked at the clinic, but now she also helped Marcus with the business — keeping books, organizing appointments, dreaming big right beside him.

"Second Chance Repairs" grew faster than they imagined.

Marcus hired more men — most of them ex-offenders who just needed someone to believe in them the way Layla had believed in him.

"I ain't just fixing cars," he told his crew one day. "We fixing lives. Ours included."

Layla watched him with quiet pride, knowing this was exactly what God had been preparing him for all along.

The Baby Announcement

A year into their marriage, Layla stood in the kitchen holding a small white stick, her breath trembling.

She'd taken three tests just to be sure — all positive.

When Marcus came home that evening, sweaty and smiling from work, she handed him a small envelope with shaking hands.

He frowned playfully. "What's this? A bill?"

"Open it," she whispered.

Inside was a sonogram photo.

Marcus stared at it for a long second, his expression unreadable — then he looked up, eyes wide, and whispered, "For real?"

Layla nodded, tears streaming. "You're gonna be a daddy."

He dropped to his knees, hands on her belly, laughing and crying all at once. "You serious? God, you serious right now?"

She laughed through her own tears. "Guess He thought we could handle one more blessing."

He looked up at her, voice breaking. "Nah, this ain't just a blessing. This is legacy."

They held each other right there in the kitchen, surrounded by the smell of dinner burning on the stove and the sound of two hearts learning how to dream again.

Peace After the Storm

Months later, on a warm spring night, Marcus sat on the porch with Layla's head resting against his chest, one hand on her belly, the other holding hers.

"You ever think about how wild this ride been?" he asked softly.

She smiled. "Every day. But I wouldn't change a single part of it."

"Not even the hard parts?"

She shook her head. "Especially the hard parts. That's where we found out what real love looks like."

He kissed her forehead, eyes glistening. "You still my reason."

"And you still my peace."

Fireflies danced across the yard as the world around them settled into quiet.

They had waited, they had prayed, and they had survived.

And now, at last, they were living the kind of love most people only dream about — the kind worth waiting for.

"The Life We Built" — the warm, soulful close to *Holding It Down: A Love Worth Waiting For.*

This is the quiet victory after years of storms — a glimpse into the peace, laughter, and family Marcus and Layla fought to earn.

Three years later, the morning sun poured through the kitchen window like honey — golden, slow, and full of grace.

Layla stood at the stove, flipping pancakes with one hand and balancing a sleepy toddler on her hip with the other. The smell of butter and maple syrup drifted through the air, mixing with gospel music playing low in the background.

"Micah, you can't keep stealing strawberries off the counter," she said, laughing as her son giggled and stuffed another one in his mouth.

"Daddy said I can!" he announced proudly, his little curls bouncing.

Marcus appeared in the doorway, coffee mug in hand and that same boyish grin that still melted her heart.

"Don't blame me," he said, kissing her cheek. "You know he's his mama's child — got good taste."

Layla rolled her eyes, smiling. "Good taste, huh? Wait till you clean up the sugar he just spilled."

Marcus scooped Micah up, tossing him playfully into the air. "Man, you making messes already? You gon' be just like your daddy — wild, handsome, and lucky enough to have a woman that keeps you in check."

Layla laughed. "If he's lucky."

The Rhythm of Everyday Love

Their home was full of life — laughter, toys, and the kind of small chaos that comes with love that's fully lived-in.

Nothing was perfect, but everything was right.

After breakfast, Layla got ready for her day — now running a small online boutique called *Lay of Grace.* Her designs, inspired by resilience and womanhood, had grown a loyal following. "Clothing for women who've survived," her slogan said — and it was more than business. It was testimony.

Marcus kissed her goodbye before heading to *Second Chance Repairs,* which now employed five full-time workers — all men he'd personally mentored. The garage walls were covered in photos of cars, families, and handwritten quotes from Marcus himself:

> *"Your past don't define you — your rebuild does."*

When he walked in, Rico was already there, music blasting.

"Boss man!" Rico shouted. "You know the city inspector's coming today?"

Marcus grinned. "Already ready for him. Let's show 'em how far we came."

He never forgot where he'd been — but he no longer lived there.

The Sunday Routine

Every Sunday was sacred. Church in the morning. Family dinner in the evening. No matter how busy life got, they made time for gratitude.

At church, Marcus sat with one arm around Layla and the other holding Micah, who often fell asleep before the sermon ended. The congregation loved them — not as a story, but as a living example of what grace could do.

Afterward, they'd gather with friends at the park — the same one where he'd proposed. Maya, now in college, would tease them about being "too cute," but everyone could see the truth: their love hadn't faded. It had just matured, deepened, rooted itself into something unshakable.

A Quiet Night

One warm evening, after Micah was asleep, Layla and Marcus sat on their porch swing, sipping sweet tea and watching the stars.

"Remember when we used to dream about this?" Layla asked softly.

Marcus nodded. "Yeah. Back when all we had was letters and hope."

She smiled. "Now look at us — a business, a family, a future."

He reached over, brushing his thumb across her hand. "You gave me all of that. Every piece."

She shook her head. "No, baby. We gave it to each other."

The porch light glowed behind them, the cicadas hummed their night song, and for a long while, they just rocked in silence — two souls who'd walked through fire and found peace on the other side.

Finally, Marcus whispered, "You ever think about how love changes shape?"

Layla leaned her head on his shoulder. "Yeah. It starts loud — passion, pain, fire — and then one day it just… gets quiet. But that quiet don't mean it's gone. It means it's home."

He kissed her forehead, eyes warm with peace. "Then I'm home for good."

The Legacy

Years later, long after people stopped talking about *the man who turned his life around*, Marcus and Layla were still side by side — older, wiser, still teasing, still praying, still grateful.

Second Chance Repairs had expanded into two locations. *Lay of Grace* sponsored mentorship programs for women starting over.

And Micah — now taller, louder, full of that same fire — was already saying he wanted to "be like Daddy when I grow up."

Sometimes Layla would find Marcus standing outside the shop after closing, just looking up at the sign.

"Still hits me," he'd say.

She'd smile, linking her arm through his. "It should. You earned it."

Full Circle

One night, after locking up, Marcus and Layla walked hand-in-hand back to their car. The streetlights flickered softly, and the moon hung full overhead — like it had been watching them all along.

Marcus stopped, turning to her. "You know what's crazy?"

"What?"

He smiled. "After everything, I still feel like I just met you. Like the story's still being written."

Layla grinned, brushing his cheek. "Then let's keep writing."

They kissed under the glow of the streetlight — not desperate or hungry, but full.

The kind of kiss that says *we made it.*

And in that quiet moment, surrounded by everything they'd built, Layla whispered the words that had started it all:

"Love worth waiting for."

Marcus smiled. "And holding down forever."

Dedication

This is for all the people who never thought life would "life" — but still found the strength to get over the hump.

Acknowledgments

First and always, I thank God — for grace, for growth, and for the kind of love that doesn't quit when life gets hard.

To my family and friends who stood beside me when the world felt heavy — thank you for reminding me what holding it down really means.

COPYRIGHT

© 2025 NFINITEE BLAYZE. All rights reserved.

No part of this book may be reproduced, stored in a retrieval system, or transmitted in any form or by any means—electronic, mechanical, photocopying, recording, or otherwise—without prior written permission from the publisher.

This is a work of fiction. Names, characters, places, and events are either the product of the author's imagination or are used fictitiously. Any resemblance to actual events, locales, or persons, living or dead, is purely coincidental.

Published by N'Finite Glo

Printed in the United States of America

Made in the USA
Coppell, TX
20 December 2025

64649583R00134